VAMPIRE DESTINY

AN EROTIC VAMPIRE SERIES
BOOKS 1-4

ARIEL MARIE

BEFORE YOU BEGIN

TABLE OF CONTENTS

SUMMER'S DESTINY

EMELY'S DESTINY

ILENA'S DESTINY

NICIA'S DESTINY

SUMMER'S DESTINY

AN EROTIC VAMPIRE SERIES, VOL. 1

CHAPTER ONE

~ Summer ~

Summer Rayne opened her eyes and recognized nothing around her. The bedroom was masculine in décor. Dark colors covered the walls and the massive four-poster bed she lay in — definitely not hers. She sat up slowly and winced at the pounding in her head. The sheet slid away, displaying her bare breast. She gasped at the realization that she was totally naked in the bed.

What in the world?

"Who the hell would take my clothes off?" she asked aloud to the empty room.

She made her way to the edge of the bed. It took a couple of scoots just to make it. The bed was large enough to easily accommodate five grown adults. She hopped down taking the sheet with her, and wrapped it around her. She staggered with her first step, grabbing onto the column of the bed as memories flashed before her eyes.

She cried out as the pressure increased in her head. She held on tighter, trying to keep her knees from buckling. Memories of her escape assaulted her. The sounds of screams echoed throughout her head as she squeezed her eyes harder, trying to block the memories.

The hunters had come.

Hunting her people down as if they were animals, shooting them in the back as they ran. Bile tried to make its way up from her stomach as she recalled running and seeing her neighbors' bodies writhing on the ground in pain as they lay dying. The hunters had acted as if they were on the quest for animals. But they weren't animals…they were vampires.

The hunters had began their attacks on vampires, by killing every vampire leader and royal family member they could find. The vampire king's body had never been found. The vampire king, who had just taken the throne a month before, was thought to have been killed that night. Since that horrendous attack on the vampire nation, life for a vampire, the following years, grew worse.

Humans had taken back the lands, as of recent, increased in numbers and become stronger than the vampires that were once the dominate race in the food chain. Following the decimation of the vampire governing body and the disappearance of the vampire king, the humans continued to hunt them down, attempting to extinguish their race. Over the years, the humans had become very creative in their ways of killing a vampire.

The vampires had been in hiding ever since, hoping and praying for the moment the king would return to lead them against the humans. Through all of the madness, Summer had finally found a small town to settle down in. It was hidden away from the human world, and she had felt safe.

Somehow, the town had been discovered and the hunters came, attacking and killing as many vampires as they could. Summer had been one of the ones lucky enough to escape. She had run as fast as her vampire abilities would allow. The last thing she remembered before blacking out was the rising of the sun.

"Where am I?" she whispered, searching the chest of drawers for clothes.

She quickly found an oversized man's t-shirt and sweatpants. She had to fold the legs of the sweat pants a few times over before her feet were free of the long legs.

"Whoever lives here must be a giant," she muttered.

She was proud of her height, five-foot two and half. Yup, she said it, *and a half.* She wanted to take credit for every inch. She was shorter than the average female vampire, but took it all in stride. Good things came in smaller packages, was how she always thought of it.

Satisfied that she was at least covered, she made her way out of the windowless bedroom, unaware of the time. She held onto the wall of the hallway, still feeling weak. She would need to find a way to get blood soon. As a born vampire, she could consume liquids but all of a vampire's nourishments came from blood. The house was eerily quiet as she made her way into what looked to be a formal living room. Again, this room was empty.

Her ears perked up at the sound of classical music floating through the air. She walked through the kitchen and followed the music. She paused at the entryway of the family room. Oversized couches, a massive wood-burning fireplace that she could easily stand up straight in, had a crackling fire burning.

Her breath caught in her throat at the figure that slowly rose from the recliner in the corner. His massive frame made the open room seem small. His button down white shirt was left open, displaying his abdominal ridges that her fingers itched to trace. Her eyes slowly traveled up his perfectly sculpted chest and found his lips curved in a small smile before her eyes met his intense dark ones.

She cleared her throat, feeling the burn of her cheeks flushing as his eyes gave way that he knew what she was thinking. The moisture collecting at the apex of her thighs, said it all. She was totally attracted to him, her body just about went up in flames in the few seconds she had been in his presence. But, that would never be. She shook her head internally. He wouldn't want her, not a common vampire.

"My king," she said bowing her head.

CHAPTER TWO

~ Ryan ~

Ryan Valerian stared at the small vampire from across the room. It took everything he had not to rush over to her. He knew that she was aroused with just one look at him. He could tell by the way her eyes traveled up his body, how her eyes held a pleased look and how quickly her chest rose as her breaths increased.

He had found her unconscious on his property, brought her in and cleaned her up. He had been her nursemaid for the past twenty-four hours, while she slept. He had found a lump on the back of her head the size of a goose egg. Being a vampire, he knew that she would heal quickly and recover from being hit on the head. He just had to wait until she woke up.

Stripping her of her clothes had left him in a state of frustration. Her rounded curves and generous breasts had caused sweat to break out along his body as he got her out of her dirty and tattered clothing. The bruises on her body had faded before his eyes as her body healed itself. He didn't know what had happened to her, but he would get to the bottom of it.

Once he was satisfied that she was cleaned and no other injuries existed, he'd placed her in his bed, covered her up and practically ran from the room. He shouldn't have reacted to an unconscious woman like that. Hell, he couldn't even remember ever reacting to any other woman like that before. He had a hard time staying away from his room while the female slept.

There is something about this one, a voice said in the back of his head.

"Welcome back to the land of the living," he said. He ignored her greeting. *My King,* she had said. He snorted. He was no longer worthy to be called a king. Kings didn't run from adversary when it came to their people. They stood and fought to the very end, if not, died for their people.

"Thank you, Your Grace," her soft voice said. "I'm Summer."

"Please, just call me Ryan." He waved her into the room. With nighttime approaching, and he already felt the effects from the moon. "How are you feeling?" he asked, motioning her to have a seat on the couch.

"Just a little weak," she replied, her large brown eyes looking around the room. "How long was I unconscious?"

"I found you yesterday morning, right before the sun rose," he said, sitting back in his chair. "You are very lucky that I had decided to do a quick check of my property."

He sent a telepathic message to his manservant, Elliot, that their guest was awake and doing fine. He had turned Elliot into a vampire more than twenty years ago. Ryan had found Elliot bloodied, beaten, and close to death. They had only been acquaintances back then.

Elliot had been the human manservant of a vampire that Ryan had known. The night that Ryan had found him, Elliot and his vampire employer had been attacked, his employer killed, and Elliot left for dead. Once Ryan turned Elliot, he had pledged to serve Ryan. Because of Ryan had sired Elliot, they would always share a telepathic link.

That is fantastic, sir. Will you be needing my service? Elliot responded.

We're fine for now.

He gripped the chair arms tight as he gazed at Summer, and fighting the urge to grab her from the couch and bend her over the back of it. He knew that she was bare beneath the shirt and pants, and that didn't help him at all right now. His cock strained against his jeans. He wasn't sure why he felt this uncontrollable urge to pound it into her until they both were deliciously sated. He would

9

need to find some relief soon.

Shit! Get a hold of yourself!

It had been a while since he had had the pleasure of losing himself in a woman. When the urge would hit, he would go into town and pick up a woman at one of the local bars who would be more than willing to come back for a night of pleasure with him. In the morning, he would use his vampiric powers to distort the woman's memories. He always let them remember the night of passion but never where he lived or who he was. He'd had to live in solitude for the past ten years and couldn't take the chance of being discovered.

"Thank you, Ryan," she said softly. He closed his eyes briefly, loving the way that his name rolled off her tongue. He needed her to say it again. Next time, he promised himself, she would scream it.

"You are welcome," he said. "Where did you come from? Not too many people know this area or travel this direction."

"I don't know," she answered, shifting her hair away from her face. He loved the deep auburn color, and how silky it looked. He was sure that by tonight, he would need a new chair by the grip he had on the arms. "My town was attacked. So much was going on and it was hard to see with all of the smoke from the homes that were set on fire."

He frowned at her story. Attacks? What attacks? He was sure if a small vampire town was attacked near him, he would have heard it.

"Summer, where are you from?" he asked.

10

"Davenport."

"Davenport is almost four hundred miles from here," he frowned. "How could you have traveled that far?"

"I was being chased." She shook her head, her eyes wide in disbelief. "The hunters were behind me. I had to keep running. I used my vampiric speed as long as I could, but they used their helicopters to track me and it took me a while before I was able to lose them."

He watched as she swayed a little on the couch. He cursed, forgetting that she hadn't had any blood in almost two days.

"Summer, come here," he commanded, unbuttoning his wrist cuff. He pushed up his sleeve to offer her his wrist. He was a strong vampire and could go days without feeding but a regular vampire could not.

"Are you sure?" she asked. "I'm sure that I could go out and hunt down an animal or something." She sat on the couch with her hands clenched in front of her.

"Nonsense," he snapped. He grimaced on the inside. *An animal?* He motioned for her to come to him. Human or vampire blood would have her feeling better, but his blood, the blood of a vampire king, would immediately return all of her strength.

He was the last of his line, the last Valerian, rulers of the vampires. The Valerians had ruled for as long as there had been documentation of vampires in the history books. And he was the first vampire king to have failed his race.

CHAPTER THREE

~ Summer ~

"It's okay," he said, his dark eyes remained on her as she stood to make her way to him. "My blood will give you back the strength you need and more."

Summer trembled on the inside. She knew that she needed blood from the starvations pains she was experiencing in her abdomen. She knelt at his feet as he offered her the sustenance that they both knew she needed.

She was still in awe that the long-lost king that was her rescuer. It had been ten years since he was last seen. Everyone knew of the Valerians and their role in leading the vampires. He was the last of his family and in order to save their race, he would need to come out of hiding.

He presented his wrist as her gums burned from her descending fangs. She gripped his wrist and brought it to her lips. Her incisors pierced his flesh, taking in his coppery nourishment. The taste of his blood was sweeter than regular blood and gave her an instant power rush.

Her body flushed as she swallowed his royal blood. Her breaths came in rapid succession as she continued to feed from him. The pains disappeared, her head no longer ached, and the small lump at the base of her neck vanished, as her body finished the healing process. She sat up on her knees, gripping his wrist tighter as the need to consume him filled her.

"That's enough, Summer," he gasped, sitting back in his chair. He pulled his arm away, leaving her wanting more.

She gasped for breath, trying to get control of herself. He may have healed all of her aches and bruises, but now, she was left still very much aroused with a pulsating pussy that was aching for release. She gripped his leg as her eyes traveled up his body, finding that he was just as shaken as she was.

Her gaze locked on his as she shifted to kneel between his legs. His eyes darkened as she ran her hands up his jean-encased legs. The muscles in his legs clenched tight as she reached the growing bulge in his pants. Her eyes didn't leave his as she made quick work of his jeans.

"Summer," his voice strained as she reached

inside of his jeans, grasping his length, and brought it out. A sigh released from her at the sight of his thickened length.

A growl escaped his throat as she caressed his thick cock with her hand. She leaned forward, running her tongue along his long length, tasting him. She groaned, sliding the mushroom tip of his thick cock into of her mouth as she continued to run her hands along him. His hands threaded their way into her hair as she took him deeper inside of her mouth.

"Fuck," he growled as she continued her sensual assault on him.

Her core clenched as he began to thrust his hips, forcing his cock deeper into her mouth. Her hand tightened it's grip as she continued to stroke him in perfect rhythm with her mouth. He leaned back in his chair with a hiss as she cradled his testicles with her free hand. They drew up close to his body signaling that he was close.

He continued to fuck her mouth and she loved every moment of the feel and the salty taste of him. With each thrust of his hips, she sucked harder and tightened her grip. Her pussy throbbed, aching to be stretched and filled by him.

"Stop," he gasped. He pulled her gently by her hair as his cock slowly slid out of her mouth.

She sat back on her heels, waiting, as he stood. She reached for him again, not ready to be done with him yet. He reached down with his hand and helped her stand. He gazed down at her and her heart skipped a beat as he trailed his fingers lightly along her jawline. Never before had she felt this strong magnetic attraction to anyone, much less had sex with someone on the first night of meeting him.

There was something about him.

She couldn't explain it. It almost felt as if she had been missing the other half of her soul, and had now found it.

In the vampire king.

He gripped the bottom of her shirt, lifting it over her head, displaying her heavy breasts. He tweaked her left nipple as he crushed his mouth to hers. He dominated her with his kiss, coaxing her tongue to duel with his as he gripped her neck, holding her steady against him as he finished disrobing her, leaving her totally naked for him to see.

She could feel the moisture seep out of her core as he looked his fill. Every inch of her body tingled as his eyes traveled up her body. She was practically trembling and he hadn't even touched her yet.

He took her hand and guided her over to the couch, leaning her over the arm of the oversized leather couch.

"Spread your legs," he murmured, directing her. She anxiously followed his directions, unable to catch her breath since her heart was pounding away in her chest. She felt open and exposed, waiting for him in this position. Her anticipating grew as she lay there, waiting for him, causing her pussy to leak even more. The cool air in the room caused her to shiver, goosebumps spread along the back of her legs as she waited. She could feel him kneel behind her.

He began his slow torture by tracing her plump labia with one finger. He slowly dipped it inside of her center, eliciting a moan from her. He nipped her ass cheek with his teeth as she wiggled her ass, waiting for him to do more.

"Hold still," he said, nipping her again with his sharp incisors.

"I can't help it," she gasped. The expectation of what was to come almost killed her. Her breasts grew heavy and she could feel moisture coat the inside of her thighs. Every inch of her tingled, waiting for the king to put her out of her misery.

Summer moaned, as she felt a second finger slide inside of her. Spreading her legs as wide as she could, she present herself to him completely. She silently cursed as her slick pussy literally throbbed, waiting with anticipation, for him to push his massive cock inside of her.

She jerked as she felt his mouth cover her pussy from behind. He gripped both of her legs, holding them in place as his tongue dove inside of her.

"Ahh…" she almost screamed as he repeatedly sucked on her clit, tugging on it gently.

He continued his assault on her pussy, rotating between sucking and licking her. Her legs continued to tremble and she wasn't sure how much longer she would be able to hold this position. If she fell over dead right now, she would die a satisfied vampire.

Her nails gripped the couch as he spread her ass cheeks apart to allow him to run his tongue from her pussy to her anus, circling her dark hole with his tongue. Her body literally vibrated under his touch. Summer's nipples were hard as diamonds as they pushed into the couch. She stood balanced on her tiptoes, trying to ensure the king could reach every aspect of her that he wanted.

He pushed his tongue deep in her pussy; at the same time, she felt a pressure from her anus as he slid his thumb inside of her dark hole. She let loose a scream as she went into a sensation overload. Waves of her orgasm crashed through her, over and over just as her body went limp.

CHAPTER FOUR

~ Ryan ~

It took everything that he had to stand. The smell and taste of Summer was a new addiction for Ryan. He would not be able to get enough of her. She whimpered as he probed her drenched pussy lips with the head of his erection. He slid his cock slowly inside of her. Sweat beaded on his forehead as he fed her every inch of him.

"Oh. My. God," she groaned as he continued.

Her slick walls gripped him and he had to pause for a second. She rotated her hips and he had to grip them to hold her in place. Never before had his body reacted like this. He breathed in deep, trying to keep his body from shooting off too early.

"Don't do that," he hissed, about to lose what little control that he had left.

He continued until he was fully seated deep within her. His dick fit perfect inside of her tight sheath. She sat up on her elbows, shifting their position where they were joined. It seemed as if the new position allowed him to slide further inside of her. He pulled out and thrust deep, slamming into her, losing the last shred of his control.

His thrusts were hard and deep as he continued to assault her pussy with his aching cock. They both moaned simultaneously as she shifted her hips. His breaths came quick as a tingling sensation gathered at the base of his balls as she met him for every motion. His fingers found their way to her hair and gripped tightly as he continued to pound away inside of her. He let loose a roar as he spewed his release inside of her as her pussy milked him.

There was no way he would let her go. He had heard of vampires having destined mates and never believed in it before. His parents' marriage was arranged, as was his grandparents. This connection with Summer had him at a loss for words. He did know one thing—she belonged with him.

"You have to come out of hiding, my king," Summer's soft voice broke the silence.

He didn't turn from the window as he stared off into the night. She had dozed off on the couch after their intense lovemaking. He refused to call what they did anything else. This small vampire had come into his life like a hurricane, wrecking everything—but for the better.

"I don't know if I can be the king that our people need," he admitted honestly. Shame filled him as he thought of how he had lived in hiding for the past decade.

Ten years ago when he disappeared, the hunters had come and destroyed everything that he had held dear. His family, security, and servants, all were killed by the human hunters. So he did what every other vampire did—ran for his life.

He was disgusted with himself. No king before him would have run. His father, had he still lived, would have stood his ground.

"Vampires need you," she said. He turned and found her standing behind him, wrapped up in the blanket he had used to cover her as she napped. "We need our king. There are plenty of vampires still willing to fight for you. We have been waiting for your return."

"I failed my people," he snapped as anguish settled in. The humans had come with weapons advanced enough to render any fight that the vampires would try useless. "It is best for our people to stay hidden."

"Hiding is not what is best for us," she snapped as she grabbed his arm to turn him toward her. "We need our king. The entire vampire race has prayed and waited for the day you would return. The minute you make your return, the entire vampire race will have your back. They will unite together as one."

"But I ran, like a coward—"

"You ran so that you could fight another day," she replied, cutting him off. "No one blamed you for running. We all did it. Over the last ten years, vampires have scattered around the world, hiding to stay alive."

Ryan stared down at her, seeing the truth in her eyes. It was his destiny to be king. He remembered his mother telling him that the stars had lined up perfectly on the night he was born and she knew that one day, he would be a great king to their people.

His mother had a way of knowing certain things about the future. She had also said that one day a female would storm into his life and flip him on his ass. He had laughed at the time, but now as he stared down at Summer, his mother's words rang clear inside his head.

It appeared that the time for him to take his throne back and lead his people against the hunters had come. It was time for the vampires to stop running. Vampires were the stronger race, true hunters and it should be them pursuing the humans, vampires food source.

Decades ago, the two races were able to live together in peace. The peace was shattered by multiple attacks on both races with the opposite blaming the other, leading to increased tension. Then the human military produced their new enhanced weapons and everything changed.

"It is time," he said slowly, reaching up to brush her dark hair away from her face. "For me to take my rightful place again."

Summer nodded, leaning into his hand as he trailed his finger alongside her face toward her neck. "They need you," she whispered.

"What about you?" he asked. He knew that they had only just met, but something deep down in his gut told him that she was the one for him. No one else would do. One taste of her and he knew he couldn't let her go.

"I need you too," she said, moving closer to him. "But right now, our people need you more."

"It is time for me to take back what is mine," he whispered against her lips while he removed her blanket. "But there is only one thing that I want— no, need."

"What is that?"

"You by my side."

CHAPTER FIVE

~ Summer ~

"I have made a few phone calls, sir," Ryan's manservant said from his bedroom doorway. Her clothes were not salvageable, but somehow Elliot had some clean new ones in her size waiting for her on Ryan's bed.

"What did you find out?" Ryan asked as he continued to pack a duffle bag. Summer sat on the edge of the bed and watched him. She could see that he was nervous. His return was needed so that their people would have a chance at life. The way they had been living the past decade was no way to exist.

"Norrix is still alive, sir," Elliot said.

"He is?" Ryan asked in disbelief. "But I thought that all of my guards were killed that night."

"It would appear that he is still alive and so are a few others. According to my contacts, they have maintained your family's home, waiting for your return."

Ryan stared at Elliot before his eyes flashed to her for a brief moment, before he zipped his bag.

"Looks as if I'm heading home," he stated, his voice hollow, as he stared down at the bag.

"The vampires just need to know that you have returned and they will rise to fight for you," she said as she hopped down off the bed and made her way to him. "You are our king," she said, placing her hand on his arm.

She didn't know what this was between them. Destiny must have placed Ryan in her path on purpose. She was sure he was meant for her and her for him. She had prayed for the day she would meet *the* one. Life had been lonely, only living for the moment, running, always having to look behind her, and never knowing when the hunters would come.

Ryan's tortured dark eyes stared at her hand before slowly moving up to meet her gaze. "What have you done to me?" he asked, covering her hand with his. "You've been here for twenty-four hours and you have upturned my life. You have me wanting to make the world a better place."

"I see a king before me," she whispered, staring up into his eyes. "A king that is worthy of the love his people are dying to give."

"Elliot," he called out, not releasing her from his

gaze.

"Yes, sir?"

"The car," Ryan said, a small smile appearing on his lips.

"It's already been pulled around to the front, sir."

Summer watched the scenery fly by as Elliot expertly navigated the roads, driving them to their destination. Since leaving Ryan's hidden home, there had been no sightings of the hunters. Summer was slightly nervous, not knowing what was to be expected. She had been used to living away from human civilization for so long, but now they were headed straight to the Valerian mansion, located near one of the largest cities that had housed humans and vampires.

The Valerian mansion had been around for centuries and still stood to this day. The massive structure was a symbol of ancient history, power, and hope for vampires all over the world.

She peeked a look at Ryan, who had yet to let go of her hand , as they sat in the back seat of the sleek expensive sedan.

"Are you nervous?" she asked.

"No." He gave her hand a squeeze. "I should have done this a long time ago."

"Are you sure you need me at your side?" she asked quietly. What he was about to embark on would not leave time for anything that she had been imagining since their night together. He had an entire race to save. She had no idea what he expected from her but deep in her heart, she knew that somehow, this vampire next to her was to be in her future.

"Yes." He turned to her and brought her hand up to his lips to place a small kiss on the back of it. "From now on, you are to remain at my side."

CHAPTER SIX

~ Ryan ~

Gasps filled the air as Ryan stalked through the front doors of his family's ancient home. The mansion had seen better days. Gone were the days of luxury in this home. Now it housed displaced vampires, which left little in the means of décor expenses. The hallways were lined with vampires who must have camped out in the building.

"Oh my God—"

"Could it be?" Excited voices whispered as he walked down the main hallway, pulling Summer behind him. Chatter increased as he led her through his family's home. Anger filled his chest at the thought of what his people had been reduced to.

If Elliot had been correct, then the head of his

security would still be here. Norrix Buchner, his faithful friend and security advisor, would ensure that the vampiric symbol of their people would remain standing. He turned a corner, walking toward the center of the house. It may have been ten years since he last set foot in the building, but he still knew the layout like the back of his hand.

He stopped dead in his tracks at the sight of four male vampires standing in the hallway. Summer crashed into his back with a gasp. He stood still as he stared at the vampires. He could feel Summer quietly peek around him.

"I'll be… fuck! Ryan, is that you?" Norrix swore, moving swiftly toward him.

"Norrix," Ryan said as the large vampire lifted him up in a bear hug, forcing Ryan to release Summer's hand.

"How the fuck have you been?" Norrix asked, putting Ryan back on the ground. "And who is this pretty little thing that you've brought with you? If this is the reason you have been gone for so long, then I would have to say—"

"I'm good," he said, cutting off his longtime friend. "This is Summer."

"Hi," she said, holding onto his arm as the other vampires approached.

"Your Grace," Remus, another of his vampire guards, greeted him as he and the others bowed before him. "We have waited for the day of your return."

"We refused to believe that you were killed,"

Zeke's deep voice chimed in. "We have protected the Valerian manor in your absence."

"I appreciate it," Ryan said, looking around at the vampires. "We have much to discuss and catch up on. My absence has been too long. It is time for the vampires to take back our rightful place back in this world."

Night slowly gave way to day by the time Ryan finally finished meeting with his vampires. He quietly made his way into his bedroom and shut the door. The black out drapes, that covered the windows, blocked the rays of the morning sun, protecting them.

Throughout the night, they had discussed what happened the night of the hunters' attack and the whereabouts of all of the remaining vampire dignitaries. They began planning their attack on the hunters. The mansion buzzed with excitement at the news of his return.

In order to try to keep the humans from discovering Ryan's return, they would not be able to use modern technology. They had to resort to communication methods of the past— foot messengers. Runners were sent to the larger hidden vampire towns to spread the word of his return.

Ryan had to admit that Summer had been right. Once vampires heard of his return, they flocked to the mansion to just get a glimpse of him. Loyal servants of the Valerian's had remained at the mansion, waiting for the day that their king would return. The house servants attended to the hundreds who came, ready to fight for not only him, but for vampires everywhere.

It had been hours since he had laid eyes on Summer. The last time he had seen her she was in the midst of helping with the displaced vampires throughout the house. She looked worn down, with dark bags beneath her eyes. She had worked nonstop since they arrival. He'd had a servant show her to his room so that she could get cleaned up and rest.

He stood over her sleeping form and knew that she was destined for him, the mate that he didn't think would ever be presented to him. His mother would have loved her. She appeared angelic as she slept with her dark hair, like a dark cloud, spread out against the crisp white pillowcases.

He needed her.

His fingers traced her flawless skin on her face, from her eyebrow to her plump lips that parted as his finger lingered on her lower lip. His cock stirred in his pants as his finger continued to make its way down her body. She slept in one of his button-down shirts, but she never buttoned it, leaving her soft breasts exposed.

His finger pushed the lapels aside, so he could take in her beautiful naked body. Her large mounds, narrowed waist, and hairless pussy, had him shucking his clothes off in record time. His gums burned as his fangs begged to descend. He needed to be inside of her now. He climbed into the bed and was pleased how she automatically turned to him as if her body sought his.

He pulled her over to him, taking off the shirt in the process. He rose over her body, and again it responded as if he had commanded it to. Her legs spread open, allowing him to settle in between her moist valley. Her eyes finally fluttered open.

"Ryan," she gasped as he took one of her breasts into his mouth. He needed to taste all of her, to consume her. He would make her his on this night. He laved the dark nipple, squeezing the mound that filled his large hands perfectly. He gently nipped and licked his way down her body, memorizing every facet of her curvy frame.

"You are already soaked for me," he said. He spread her moist folds, finding her pussy, soaked with her desire for him. He nipped her inner thigh as she moaned his name again. "Say my name again," he demanded, needing to hear his name on her lips. He wanted the whole world to hear her scream his name.

"Ryan, please," she begged, grinding her pelvis as he traced her pussy lips with his fingers. He loved looking at her pink perfection. This belonged to him. He inserted one finger inside of her drenched opening, while licking her sensitive bud. He felt her body shudder as he played with it. He wanted her body writhing along the bed, to give her the greatest pleasure that she would ever experience.

"This pussy belongs to me," he growled, inserting two fingers now into her tight channel.

"Oh, God—"

He covered her pussy with his mouth, sucking on her slick mound while he continued to finger fuck her. He continued his motions with his fingers while alternating between sucking on her clit and flicking it with his tongue. Her legs spread wider as he consumed all of her pussy.

Summer's liquid sweetness continued to pour out of her, coating his face and made him even harder. He got pleasure out of knowing that he brought her to the brink of an orgasm. He kept his eyes on her as her body jerked and shook while he suckled her. Her fingers threaded their way into his hair and pulled him closer as she thrust her pussy against his mouth.

"Yes," she groaned, continuing to thrust her pussy against his tongue, moaning his name repeatedly.

He could feel her muscle bunch up as she let loose a scream. He clamped down on her clit and sucked harder. She tried to scoot away from him but he grabbed her legs to hold her in place.

"Never run from me," he said, as climbed his way back up her body.

He grabbed her face, covering her mouth with his as he thrust his tongue into of her mouth, claiming it as he had her pussy. He lined up his cock with her entrance and thrust deep.

"Say that you are mine," he demanded as he turned her head away from him in order to expose her jugular vein to him.

"I belong to you."

He sank his incisors into her pounding artery. His mouth instantly filled with her blood as he continued to thrust his length inside of her tight pussy. Her thick blood was pure, sweet, and addictive. He quickened his thrusts, holding her tight to him as the waves of his orgasm crashed into him. He released her throat, roaring his release as he poured all of himself inside of her.

He caught himself from crashing down onto Summer. He stared down into her eyes before turning his neck to offer himself to her. She sat up, flashing her small fangs just before grabbing his hair, claiming him as hers.

CHAPTER SEVEN

~ Summer ~

"Good morning, Your Grace," a small voice appeared behind Summer. She still had to get used to being addressed as royalty. It had been two weeks since their mating, making her Ryan's for all eternity and the new queen of the vampires.

"Yes," she turned, finding Lucilla, the head servant, behind her. Lucilla and Summer had been working close to ensure that vampires that came to the Valerian mansion were not turned away and were provided with provisions, and a safe place to lay their head during the day.

"There is a vampire who states that he is from Davenport, demanding that he speak to you." Lucilla looked concerned as she wrung her hands. "Do you want me to get one of the guards?"

Summer was stunned. She didn't know who would have survived the massacre that night, much less, be looking for her. She hesitated at first, but disregarded the feeling. The security at the Valerian mansion was impenetrable. If she was able to escape the hunters that night, she was sure it probably was another vampire who had been able to get away too.

"If it's a vampire that survived the Davenport massacre, then I'm sure it should be fine," she said. "I'm sure it's just someone looking for a safe place to lay his head. Where is he?"

"He's on the garden veranda, Your Grace," Lucilla said as Summer headed in that direction.

After helping so many vampires find safe areas to stay, she was sure that this was probably the same request. Davenport had been a small community where everyone looked out for each other. She was still saddened by the thought that her neighbors and friends were dead.

Summer pushed open the do that led out to the back of the house that led to the gardens. Dusk had just settled, as the sun disappeared beneath the horizon. Her eyes adjusted to the low light outside as she made her way to the gardens. She walked up the veranda not seeing anyone. Summer frowned; she was sure that Lucilla had told her the guest was on the garden veranda.

She turned to go back to the house and jumped, finding a large figure standing behind her. Summer's eyes narrowed, focusing on the figure and realizing it was a human. She gasped as someone grabbed her from behind.

"Let me go," she screamed, as she struggled to get free, but the arms tightened around her.

"It's her," a voice growled as they covered her mouth with a foul smelling cloth.

"No, let me go," she tried to scream again but this time, she faded into darkness.

"Wake up, vampire," a voice growled in Summer's ear.

Summer struggled to get her eyes to obey and open. She groaned; her head felt as if it was stuffed with cotton balls. She rolled her head, finally able to get her eyes to open. Two human males stood in the windowless room, watching her. One of the two, she recognized from the massacres from her town, the other one she had never seen before. She would recognize the scar that ran down the left side of his face anywhere. He had been there the night the Davenport massacre happened. She would remember the look on his face for the rest of her life. He took great pleasure in killing vampires.

"Do you know how long we have chased you, little vampire?" Scarface growled, grabbing her by her hair and pulling her into a sitting position on the couch. Her wrists had been cuffed in front of her and she flopped back on the couch, unable to get her balance on the edge of the cushion.

"What do you want?" Summer asked, wincing on the inside. She didn't want to display any type of weakness. She knew the human hunters would not hesitate in killing her.

"The vampire you've been fucking," the other male snapped. Her stomach rolled from the thought that these two animals had been a witness to every intimate moment that she had shared with her mate.

"We've been watching you," Scarface sneered. "You may have run from us, little vampire, but you led us directly to the vampire we have been hunting for years."

Summer silently cursed herself. She had thought that she had lost them. She had exhausted herself from using her vampire speed for so long. By the time she lost consciousness, she was sure that no one would have been able to find her.

"Who would have thought?" the other male asked. "That the pretty little vampire slut would have led us to their fucking king."

"He won't deal with anyone but your leader," she rushed out. She didn't know what Ryan would do. She just tried to buy herself time to figure out a way to escape. The hunters never let vampires live once they captured them. Summer figured she had escaped them once before, and she would have to do it again.

"He'll speak to me," a third voice appeared at the doorway to the small room. Both human males stood at attention as the newcomer entered the room. A refined older human male, with gray hair and round glasses, dressed in a military uniform stepped into the room. He exuded power the minute he stepped into the room and Summer could tell he was used to being in charge. "So this is the vampire who escaped from Davenport?"

"Yes, sir," Scarface said, looking straight ahead as the older man eyed her.

"What is your relationship to the vampire king?" the older human asked, his eyes cold and hard as he stared at her.

As she looked at the humans, she knew that she would never give Ryan over to the hunters. She had grown to care for him too much. He was her mate; the other half of her soul that she never knew was missing. He was the king of her people. He would make a stand against these hunters. She realized then just how much she loved him.

She would die for him.

CHAPTER EIGHT

~ Ryan ~

"The hunters have her," Ryan growled to the vampires in his office. It had been close to twenty-four hours since Summer was last seen. Ryan paced the room as his imagination ran free with the possible situations that Summer could be in.

His mate had been snatched right from under his nose. His heart almost stopped when Lucilla ran to him screaming that hunters had kidnapped their queen. Lucilla proceeded to inform him of how a vampire had told her that he was looking to speak to the queen in private.

According to Lucilla, Summer believed that it was a vampire from her old town and she went to meet the vampire alone. He closed his eyes briefly, loving that his mate had a big heart for her people.

But by the time Lucilla and the guards had gone to the veranda, there were no trace of Summer.

"We will get her back, my king," Norrix promised fiercely. Even in the short time that Ryan had spent with Summer, in his family's home, every vampire had come to love her.

"Every vampire in the country is ready to fight," Zeke said. "Everyone is in position as we have planned."

Ryan and his vampires had quickly come up with a plan to attack the hunters. In the past two weeks, vampire across the world had stepped up and coordinated attacks on all of the hunters' bases of operation. Once the bases around the world were taken out, the hunters wouldn't have any ground to stand on.

"They are waiting on your call," Zeke said, breaking through Ryan's thoughts. It was time to take back what was theirs.

"Make the call," he said. "Level them to the ground. I want them to scramble, to run and try to hide. Destroy the hunters," he growled turning back to the room.

"Yes, Your Grace," Zeke said, picking up the telephone on the desk near him.

"Remus, I want—"

"My king!" a voice yelled before the door burst open with a young vampire boy. "Santos sent me to find you. The hunters have been spotted on their way here!"

"Thank you, my child," Ryan nodded to the

boy. "Rizzo, have Santos ready the guards."

"Yes, sir!" Rizzo took off running, leaving the room as fast as he blew in.

"We shall go meet the hunters in battle," Ryan commanded as he continued to pace the floor. Growls echoed around the room, signaling that they were all ready to dive straight into battle to save their queen and take back the world in which they live in.

His feelings for Summer had awakened those profound qualities of the king that was buried deep inside of him, hidden beneath his shame for failing his people. Because of Summer that shame no longer existed inside of him. Because of Summer, his eyes were opened. Her love that made him see, that his people needed him. She needed him. It was time for him to become the vampire king that Summer believed him to be.

~Summer~

The woods were too quiet. The human hunters hadn't picked up on the fact that there were no sounds of animals, or life around them. There was a dead silence as if the forest creatures had run away knowing something dangerous approached. She knew the vampires were coming for her.

Her lover, her mate, her king, was coming for her.

Ryan wouldn't let her die by the hands of the

hunters. She smiled on the inside knowing that her vampire king was coming and would kill these hunters.

The hunters had not realized that they had finally pushed the vampires past their breaking point. Vampires, who had been pushed into a corner, threatened to the point where they had no choice, would finally react. The entire vampire race joined together, ready to attack. No longer would vampires be hunted down. The vampires would fight and claw their way back to the top of the food chain.

She held in a groan as they tied her to a post in the middle of the woods. The ropes bit into her wrist as she was placed on display. They had tortured her, trying to get information out of her about the vampire king, but she would have rather died than give in. Gashes lined her body as they had bled her, leaving her in a weakened state.

She looked to the sky, taking in the paleness of the sky. Sunrise would be here soon. She had every confidence that Ryan and his vampires would save her before the sun could rise. If they didn't make it soon, she would be in big trouble. The sun-rays would burn her skin and in her weakened state, she would be burned alive.

"We're going to call the bloodsucker's mansion and let him know we have his prize," Scarface said to the leader. She looked around at them, noting that they had their enhanced weapons on them.

Those weapons were the reason that the humans

were able to kill so many vampires, sending them running. They didn't have to use wooden stakes anymore. These newer weapons were deadlier than any wooden stake would ever be.

The humans' military scientist had been able to develop a chemical that mimicked the effects sun's light and instill it into bullets. Solis, named after the sun, was deadly to vampires. Once the chemical entered a vampire's blood stream, it would kill them within minutes, burning them from the inside out as their heart pumped the chemical throughout their body.

"You do that," the leader chuckled, holding his enhanced gun in his hand. "They don't have much time; the sun will be rising soon. Looks like we are going to have us an old-fashioned vampire burning this morning."

The men chuckled, walking around the small clearing while Scarface placed a call on his cell phone, but Summer knew that it would be pointless.

The vampires were near.

She could feel them. She closed her eyes, thanking the Gods that they were close. She really didn't feel like burning alive today.

"No one answered, sir," Scarface said, placing his cellphone into his pocket.

"Well, it looks like your king won't be showing up. Leave you to burn by sunlight today," the leader sneered. "How's that for your lover boy?"

"Do you think that they would just sit by and

wait by the phone to hear from you?" she barked a short laugh, unable to believe that they would think that the vampires would be waiting for a phone call. The leader's face straightened as he stalked to her.

"Laugh all you want," he sneered in her face. Her gums stretched and burned as her fangs descended. She needed blood and her body, starving for the coppery substance, could sense that fresh blood was near. "The sun will be rising soon and we'll see who will be laughing as the sunlight hits your skin."

"I may die today, but I guarantee you that none of you will walk away from this," she spat. "Vampires are rising; there is nothing that you hunters can do to stop them."

"There is no one here now," he said, pointing his gun, filled with Solis bullets, directly at her heart. One bullet would be all it would take to kill her. Her heart would pump the chemical straight through her, killing her in minutes. Her eyes narrowed at him as she bared her fangs. A movement out of the corner of her eye caught her attention.

They were here!

"You're too late, hunter," Summer whispered fiercely, her lips curving into a deadly fang-filled smile, as all hell broke loose.

Ryan and his vampires converged on the clearing within seconds, killing the two flunkies before they could even draw their guns out of their holsters. The hunter's leader jumped behind her, untying her quickly, and snatched her in front of him, keeping the Solis gun placed against her temple. He was outnumbered.

He would not leave here alive.

Six fierce vampires stood in front of them as he slowly backed up with Summer in front of him.

"Don't come any closer," her captor shouted, his arm tightening around Summer's neck.

"Let her go," Ryan demanded.

"Why? She's my ticket out of here alive," the leader hollered.

"You were dead the minute you took her," Ryan hissed, his eyes narrowed on the hunter, his hands clenched into a fist.

"You vampires will die! We'll wipe out your kind. You're an abomination!"

"Right now as we speak, vampires around the world are attacking every hunter's base of operations," Ryan boasted, walking slowly towards them. The other vampires slowly spread out, encircling them. He was trapped. "We will no longer run from a hunter."

"You lie!" the leader shouted, his gun digging into the side of Summer's temple, causing her to wince. Ryan's eyes connected with her and she knew that she could trust him. "Don't move!"

"This ends today," Ryan growled.

"I will kill her!" the hunter shouted. She heard the cock of the hammer and closed her eyes. In her weakened state, he practically dragged her with him as he tried to back away from the vampires. "Just try—"

His words ended with a gurgle. Summer felt his arm relax from around her neck, falling away, and releasing her. Her body swayed, too weak from blood loss, to stand on her own. Her knees gave way as she fell forward. A set of arms caught her before her head slammed into the ground. A thud sounded behind her.

"Gotcha," Ryan whispered into her ear, cradling her to his chest.

"I knew you would come," she whispered, closing her eyes and breathing in his scent as he barked orders at the others.

"What did they do to you?" he bit out around his fangs as her eyes met his.

"Nothing that won't heal," she said softly, not wanting to upset him anymore than he already was. She wrapped her arms around his neck. She was just too tired to worry about anything now, while in the safety of his arms.

"Later," he muttered, standing with her in his arms. She knew that he would try to get her to tell him everything. "You need blood."

"Norrix," he called out.

"Yes, Your Grace," Norrix answered, appearing at Ryan's side.

"Handle this here. I need to get our queen home." She tightened her arms around his neck. His commanding tone let everyone know who was in charge.

She knew it.

The king in him would show himself. She just had a feeling that the future of vampires everywhere was about to change.

"No problem." Norrix nodded his head looking around the clearing. "It won't take long at all. We'll have to think of something clever to dispose of the hunters' bodies."

"Good; for tomorrow, we take back what was ours."

EPILOGUE

~ Ryan ~

A month had passed since the hunters had kidnapped his queen. Vampires everywhere had banded together, once again, under the Valerian name to fight for their future. Vampires attacked the human hunters with a force that had them retreating and rethinking their way of life.

Not all humans had been on the side of the hunters. Like every race, there will always be some bad apples. In the case of the humans, the vampire hunters, rose to the leadership roles in their world, brainwashing many into hunting down vampires.

The vampires destroyed the hunter bases of operations and their military facilities that made Solis and all weapons that were to be used to kill the vampires. With the destruction of the hunters, the humans began to rebuild their governments and a new way of life.

A truce had been reached between the vampires and humans. They agreed to coexist in peace once again. Tension still remained and would take some time to dissipate, but for now, the battle between the races had ceased.

Ryan walked outside to meet Summer in the garden. Even though there was a truce in place, he still didn't want to leave her unprotected. She was to have a guard with her at all times, unless he was with her. She had put up a fierce argument that she wouldn't need a guard, but this was one argument that he was glad he had won.

Their argument led to a kiss, and before long he had her moaning yes, having changed her mind once his tongue dove between her legs. He smiled to himself, now knowing what his secret weapon would be for future arguments.

He reached his mate, finding her sitting on a bench gazing into the koi pond located in the center of the garden. He nodded to the guard, dismissing him. She turned to him as he sat beside her. The moonlight highlighted her creamy skin and her bright smile. A few seconds in her presence and already, he ached for her.

"Hello," she said softly, scooting over to snuggle into the crook of his arm.

"Hey," he said pulling her close. He breathed in her fresh scent, loving everything about the way she smelled and the way she smiled. She was his everything and he would continue to fight to make the world a better place for her.

"This is only the beginning," he said, pressing his lips to the top of her head. The last month had flown by. Rebuilding a kingdom left them precious little time to spend together.

"I know," she sighed. "But this will secure our future. It will be worth it."

"I'm just thankful that destiny led you to me," he said, pulling back from her. Without her in his life, he would probably still be hidden away in his self-inflicted hell. He tipped her chin up, giving him access to her lips. "There is no one else I'd rather have at my side."

He covered her mouth with his and proceeded to show her how much he meant every word.

~The End~

EMELY'S DESTINY

AN EROTIC VAMPIRE SERIES VOL. 2

CHAPTER ONE

~ Norrix ~

Norrix Buchner silently observed his king pace the floor before him; the long lost king who had recently returned. Not only was Ryan Valerian the King of the Vampires, he was a childhood friend of Norrix's. It was because of their longtime friendship that Norrix had remained loyal to the Valerian name.

Norrix's loyalty knew no boundaries. When the human hunters attacked vampires across the world, causing Ryan to disappear into hiding, it was Norrix and a few others who had remained behind and protected the Valerian Manor. The home of the ruling vampire family was top priority. It was a symbol of hope for vampires everywhere for the last ten years.

Human scientists with the military had developed an advanced weapon called Solaris. The chemical compound, which mimicked the effects of the sun's rays, was then made into bullet form. Not long after, hunters were able to obtain these weapons. Whether on their own, or with the help of people inside the military, they set out in an attempt to decimate the lives of vampires.

Norrix growled slightly at the thought of how many vampires were lost at the hands of the human hunters.

"These humans are going to fuck us over the first chance they get," Ryan muttered, straightening to his full height.

They were about to go into a meeting with the human leaders to sign the Vampire-Human Truce Agreement. This agreement would help rebuild the relationship between vampires and humans, which had been torn apart by the Human Radical Militia Group— or, the *hunters*.

"Well, this time, if the humans attack vampires again, we will be prepared," Norrix said, looking to his fellow vampire guards. Remus and Zeke both nodded their heads in agreement.

"You're right. Vampires will never run and hide again. We will stand and fight if need be." Ryan stopped his pacing and turned to face Norrix and the other guards. "With this agreement, vampires will be safe to live their lives as they see fit. Solaris manufacturing will cease. The human leaders must agree to this truce. Vampires will rise to the top of the food chain again."

Norrix held up his hand to silence his king. Not out of disrespect, but caution. They were in a sitting room in a secured human facility, awaiting the human's security advisor's team. Norrix pointed to his ears, signaling that the room may be bugged. Ryan nodded, understanding.

"How is mated life?" Norrix asked, changing the subject. He was sure they would continue the conversation later.

"Mated life is amazing," Ryan laughed, and settled with a sincere smile on his lips. Norrix knew that it was the vampire queen, Summer, who had persuaded Ryan to come out of hiding, reclaim his throne, and defend the vampire nation as only the vampire king could. Norrix couldn't even begin to show his gratitude toward the queen for what she had done.

Vampires everywhere loved Queen Summer. She was a breath of fresh air in a world that had become darkened and filled with nothing but fear and death. She helped restore hope for all vampire kind.

"One day, I hope all of you will be blessed by the gods to find the other half of your soul," Ryan said, nodding to each of them.

Zeke scoffed. "I'll leave the falling in love to you crazy sons of bitches. Love is a fairy tale."

"Zeke!" Remus snapped, shooting daggers with his eyes at Zeke.

Norrix chuckled at the pair. He knew that the

king was in love with the queen, and teased them all about settling down. Ryan may have been gone for ten years, but Norrix still knew his friend well. Ryan's whole demeanor changed at the mention of his queen. Norrix had no problem with taking a mate, as long as he felt she was worthy.

"It's okay," Ryan said with a small smile, his hand in the air. "He's just—"

A knock sounded at the door, cutting the king off. The teasing in the room instantly dissipated as the guards went on alert. Even with the promise of a treaty signing, none of the vampires could relax fully. After all the hunters had put the vampire nation through, it would be hard for any vampire to relax in the presence of a human.

Zeke shifted silently toward the door, while Remus and Norrix both positioned themselves in front of Ryan. Zeke looked over his shoulder. Once satisfied that Ryan was protected, he opened the door.

"They will see you now," a feminine voice announced from the other side of the door. The voice belonged to Lisa, a human assistant to one of the dignitaries that Ryan was to meet with.

Norrix noticed that Zeke's body had yet to relax. He could see that his fellow vampire guard's back muscles were still tight.

"Is there a problem?" Norrix asked, moving toward Zeke.

Zeke opened the door, fully revealing a militant escort. Six humans stood there, decked out in their military tactical gear. Norrix snorted. Without their precious Solaris bullets, the humans would be no match for the vampires.

"An escort," Ryan acknowledged. "It's fine. Let's get this meeting over with.

"Your Grace, I'm sure you will find that everything is in order," the Secretary of Defense, Christopher Wayne, noted.

Norrix, along with the other vampire guards, were on high alert. In the room sat the human dignitaries with their militant bodyguards. Norrix didn't trust any of them one bit. It was the human scientists who created Solaris with the sole intent of ridding vampires from the face of the Earth.

The humans finally surrendered when the vampires had had enough. The vampires had rallied behind Ryan and retaliated with such force that the humans didn't have a choice but to give in.

As with any race, there were good, descent people, and then there were those who were pure evil.

Norrix watched as Ryan nudged the documents that lay before him on the table. He couldn't see the king's face, but he could tell that he was not happy through his body language. Ryan didn't say one word as he browsed through the treaty. Norrix glanced at Remus and Zeke, who were glaring at the human security.

"According to my wife, there are research facilities that the hunters managed," Ryan began, then looked up from the paperwork at the human dignitaries sitting across from him. "What happened to them?"

General Bruce Lawson of the human's army responded. "Those facilities were not sanctioned by the U.S. government—"

"I didn't ask if your government supported them," Ryan snapped. His voice remained calm, but it held a deadly note.

The vampires in the room shifted as they waited for their king.

"I asked what happened to them. Have they been shut down?" Ryan's voice dropped a few degrees.

Norrix shifted, his eyes locked on the humans. The soldier in the front placed his hand over the weapon at his hip. Norrix prayed he wouldn't be fool enough to reach for it. The human's eyes narrowed on Norrix as the tension in the room heightened.

"We've had no control over them. They were privately funded facilities," the Secretary of Defense stated. "You are more than welcome to check them out and see if there is anything still there."

"Oh, we will." Ryan's voice was cold as ice as he made his demands. "Until I have confirmed that every vampire has been released, this treaty will not be signed. I want the addresses to every known facility."

The room erupted with the humans' protests.

Ryan held up his hand, silencing them.

"We can do this the easy way or the hard way, that's up to you. You will give my security advisor the addresses to the facilities immediately," Ryan advised. He stood from his chair, motioning to Norrix.

Norrix and the other vampires stood behind their king. Norrix could feel his gums burning with the thought of a good fight. He refused to take his eyes off the security guards.

Bring it, Norrix thought.

It had been a few months since their last fight. The vampires had rescued the queen from the hunters, then went on a rampage, destroying the humans as they got the queen to safety.

"We will give you the addresses of all known facilities," the general conceded. He snapped his fingers once. Lisa moved from her corner of the room and provided a piece of paper from her leather portfolio.

"Thank you," Ryan said, taking the piece of paper from her. "You will hear from me once we have determined that the facilities are all shut down, non-operational in any capacity, and no prisoners remain. I'm sure that you all understand that I want what's best for my people."

Ryan stalked out of the room with Norrix, Remus, and Zeke in tow, leaving the human council members sputtering. He didn't give them a chance to reply. Norrix grinned on the inside, proud of his friend. The vampires made haste in leaving the human facility and arrived at the royal SUV.

"There are three facilities on this sheet of paper," Ryan confirmed, as Norrix held the SUV door open for him. "Summer is convinced that there are still vampires being held in them."

Once Ryan was secured inside the vehicle, Norrix slammed the door shut and jogged to the other side.

"Let's go," Norrix directed Remus as he settled into the back of the vehicle alongside Ryan. They quickly pulled out, away from the building.

"Clear the buildings," Ryan directed. "Then, I want them all burned to the fucking ground."

CHAPTER TWO

~ Emely ~

Emely knew that something was wrong. She had sat in her cell and watched as the human scientists scrambled around their workstations. Complete mayhem had consumed the testing facility as they packed up and destroyed as many files as they could. Computers and equipment were packed up and removed from the facility. It was as if the laboratory employees were trying to erase any proof of their documented experiments, or that they were ever there.

Now, in the wake of the humans hurried exit, the five vampires locked away in cells were left—*forgotten*.

Emely glanced around the abandoned lab and could see the other vampires. She walked over to the bars and sat down on the floor.

Her and the others there would probably die. There would be no one to give them the nourishing blood that they would need to survive. It was not the way she would have preferred to die. Dying of old age was the way she wanted to go, not starving in a prison cell after being a test subject for two years.

She brushed her dark hair away from her face as she continued to observe the empty lab. Aside from her, there were four other vampires; two females, two males.

Ten years ago, the human hunters turned on vampires, slaughtering them at first sight. Emely, like every other vampire, ran for her life. The hunters were a radical group of humans that were decimating the vampire population. Humans, not affiliated with the hunters, ignored what was going on—allowing it. Vampires were seen as a threat, and the hunters believed they were doing a *favor* for all humans.

Ten years ago, Emely's whole world changed. She had lost her entire family at the hands of the hunters. She smiled faintly at the memory of her papa and Mama. They'd had a strong family bond. Emely missed her parents more and more as each day passed. Life wasn't fair. They hadn't deserved to be hunted down, as if they were animals. But, neither of her parents would want her to mourn their deaths. They would want her to make the most of her life.

Her parents had owned one of the most prominent blood labs that catered to vampires. She had learned everything about her family's business with the intent of one day running one of the largest cryo labs in the country.

Her life since then had been spent being used as a lab rat by the human scientists to study. She'd been exposed to sunlight and burned, starved of blood, and all for the purpose of educating humans on a vampire's genetic makeup, looking for ways to exploit even more of their weaknesses. Other vampires were put through far worse experiments, and most did not survive.

Looking around the bleak laboratory had reality crashing down around her. She thought of how vampires were no longer the top of the food chain, and how the prey had become the hunter. But, Emely believed that one day, that would all change. She had faith that the vampires would rise again.

The vampire king had gone into hiding when the attacks from the hunters began. As time went on, word spread that King Valerian's guards were defending the royal family's home.

Stories of the guards led by the infamous Norrix reached vampires near and far. Norrix, known as one of the fiercest vampire warriors and loyal defenders of the vampire king, was a legend.

It was known that displaced vampires could go to the Valerian Manor for safety and protection. It was when Emely made the attempt to travel to the royal family home for help that she was captured.

The sound of moaning grabbed Emely's attention. She glanced over to the cell located about twenty feet away from hers.

"Hey," Emely called out. Worry filled her chest as the female moaned again, holding her stomach. "Are you okay over there?"

Emely sat up straighter as she watched the female rock back and forth on her cot.

"It's the thirst," a deep male voice answered. It was the tall dark vampire locked away in the room across from her. "The fuckers just left and didn't even have the decency to let us out."

"Goddess above, please help us," a feminine plea sounded from the other side of the lab. Her voice was laced with panic as she continued to pray aloud. "We are going to die here."

"It will be okay," Emely blurted out, wanting to comfort her. She really didn't know what else to say, and it was the first thing that came to her mind.

"In what way are we going to be okay?" the other male vampire snapped. "We are going to starve to death. She needs blood."

Emely pressed her face to the bars and stared at the female. She hated this helpless feeling. As hostages, each of them had felt their share of pain. Emely had been poked and prodded for the last two years. She was still recovering from her last torture sessions.

The scientist had just completed an extreme

experiment on her a week ago, pushing her near the threshold of death. They had wanted to test her healing capabilities while they withheld blood.

She cringed, still remembering the feel of the silver blades piercing her flesh as they continued to slice and impale her with their knives. With the extreme loss of blood and no ability to consume fresh blood, Emely was sure that she would have crossed over into the afterlife.

"What is your name?" Emely called out to the troubled vampire. She wanted to try and get her attention, but the vampire didn't answer; her moans only grew louder.

"We're going to die!" The other female's wailing grew louder also, as panic began to settle in.

"Shut up!" the first male vampire roared. "Crying and screaming is not going to save us."

"Who is going to save us?" the other male asked. "No one knows we are here!"

The walls trembled as the thrum of a helicopter landed outside. The laboratory grew silent as the vampires tried to listen. Shouting could be heard outside the windowless building.

Emely's heart pounded, as she got excited. Was it someone coming to save them? Or was it the human guards coming back for them? She stood slowly as she waited to see who would storm through the double doors of the lab.

Her breath caught in her throat as the sound of thunderous footsteps increased. She sent up a silent prayer that they were going to be rescued, and not killed by guards returning to get rid of them, once and for all.

The door to the laboratory burst open and Emely's knees threatened to give out as relief spread through her.

They were being rescued!

Vampires wearing the king's color guard on their shirts strode into the laboratory. A deep voice barked out orders as the vampires spread out to the cells. Emely's eyes locked onto the vampire in charge, and she instantly recognized him.

Her knees gave out when his piercing eyes returned her gaze as he stalked toward her. She leaned against the bars as she slid to the floor.

"Are you okay?" his deep voice rumbled.

His dark eyes were intense, as if he could see into the depths of her soul. She couldn't catch her breath. A part of herself she thought long dead began to wake up. She could feel her body respond to his in a way that warmed her cheeks as he waited for a reply from her. Her gums burned slightly from her incisors breaching through the skin.

"Are you a mute?" he asked as he signaled for someone to come over. She shook her head. As her eyes looked around the room, she found the king's guards assisting the other vampires out of their cells.

They truly were saved.

She wanted to weep with joy. No longer would she be a test subject, getting poked, prodded, and tortured.

It was over.

"What is your name?" His voice broke through her thoughts.

"Emely," she whispered, looking up to him. He was more beautiful in person than any picture she had seen of him in the past.

He was her savior.

"That's a pretty name, Emely," Norrix remarked as he accepted a tool from one of the other guards. "Emely, I need you to back up from the bars."

She did as she was told until her back bumped up against her small cot. She watched the tool release a bright beam of light that melted the lock. Norrix swung the door open and handed the tool off to the other large vampire guard before he strolled into her private cell with his larger-than-life presence. Emely watched him as he reached out a hand for her to take.

"Come with me."

CHAPTER THREE

~ Norrix ~

Seeing the helpless female vampire locked behind the prison cell almost broke him. He didn't understand what his feelings meant, but the moment he laid eyes on Emely, he realized that he would have killed any and all humans who had hurt her. Her large gray eyes had haunted his dreams ever since.

Forty-eight hours had passed since the night they rescued the vampire hostages, and he had carried Emely into the infirmary.

He had to see her again. He needed to make sure that she was all right and adjusting to life outside captivity. Norrix knew that it was silly for him to check on her, but for some reason, unbeknownst to him, he was drawn to her.

Norrix entered the busy infirmary. Queen Summer had been correct about the hidden research facilities testing on vampires. It was because of her that they were able to save the lives of five vampires. After discovering the facility that housed Emely and the other vampires, it led Norrix and Ryan to wonder how many others were detained in the other facilities.

Norrix walked through the small medical center, looking for Emely. With the rescue, the nurses and physicians had been working tirelessly around the clock.

He ambled past the one female vampire that they didn't think would have lived another day had they not made it to the research facility when they did. Menaya was her name, and the humans had been starving her. The thirst for blood had consumed her, and her body had literally begun to turn in on itself since she didn't have any fresh blood. He glanced at the bag of blood that hung on an IV pole as he passed Menaya's bed. Her eyes remained closed as she healed. He nodded to her nurse as he passed.

Finally, he found her.

Emely Winter was sitting on the side of her bed. She was dressed in a plain gray T-shirt and sweatpants. Her tiny feet were bare, and his eyes gravitated to her unpolished toenails. He swallowed hard. She may be a vampire, a strong predator by nature, but right now, her eyes gave way to her vulnerability.

This beautiful vampire should have never been behind bars. He couldn't even begin to imagine the horrors she had experienced at the hands of the humans.

Not anymore.

He would protect her.

He paused at the thought, and as her beautiful gray eyes met his, he knew that he was a goner. He would protect her with his life. She belonged with him.

"Hi," he said, stopping at the foot of her bed.

"Hello," Emely responded softly. She tucked a few strands of her hair behind her ear.

He watched, fascinated, as a warm blush spread across her cheeks. Each of the rescued vampires were brought to the infirmary to be assessed by the king's physicians. Some were still injured from their last encounters, but they were all expected to heal fully.

"I heard that you were being released by the physicians today," he began. She nodded. "I was going to escort you to your private quarters."

Her eyes widened at the announcement. He knew that she had probably assumed that she would go with the other displaced vampires that came to the king's mansion for assistance, which is something the queen had graciously set up for the vampires who needed it.

Emely wouldn't need the queen's help. He would take care of her.

Norrix owned a small property that was

adjacent to the Valerian lands. A small house that he had built for the day when he would decide to settle down. But for now, it could be hers.

***

"This is too much!" Emely exclaimed. "I could have gone where the others were placed."

"You don't like it?" Norrix asked with a frown as he gazed at the home he had built.

The house was built twenty years ago, and no one had lived in it since. Being the security advisor to the king had kept Norris extremely busy. The house was built for a family, and he just couldn't bring himself to sleep in the house alone. It didn't feel right without a mate. His quarters in the royal house allowed him to be readily available for the king.

He had arranged for a cleaning crew to come out to clean and air it out. The home hadn't been opened in the last ten years.

He tried to look at the home through Emely's eyes. It was a two story white cottage with navy blue shutters. The flowerbeds were bare, but the yard was neatly manicured.

"You said it was a small cottage. This is magnificent. It's beautiful, but I couldn't." She shook her head as she gazed longingly at the house. He could see in her eyes that she wanted to stay.

"Why are you doing this?" she asked as she

turned to him. "What do you want from me?"

"Nothing," he answered truthfully.

He would not ask anything of her; she had been a prisoner for two years. He ignored the question of why and motioned for her to follow him up the stairs onto the porch. He would tell her later. Once she was settled and healed, then he would tell her that he believed her to be his mate.

Mate.

He swallowed hard as he put the key in the door. That was a big word to throw around, and he wanted to be one hundred percent sure that she was his. It would be hard for him to believe that he would find his mate, but after watching Ryan and Summer, he knew that destined mates truly existed.

Norrix held the door open for her to enter. Emely slowly walked past him into the home. He shut the door behind him and paused, watching her explore.

He'd had the crew not only clean the house from top to bottom, but had new furniture delivered. He wanted to make it a home for her. The last ten years for vampires had been a cruel, dark world, but now that the king had returned, everything was changing for the better.

"Let me show you where you will be sleeping," he said, walking up the stairs.

"And where will you sleep?" she asked as she followed behind him.

"I have a room in the mansion," he informed her

as he opened the master bedroom door, allowing her to enter first. It was a beautiful suite with a private master bath attached.

"Oh my goodness!" she gushed, rushing into the bathroom. "I haven't had a shower in years!" Her voice echoed from the large lavatory, carried into the room and pierced his heart.

"Go ahead. There are fresh towels and toiletries in there for you," he called out.

"Will you stay here with me?" Emely asked, appearing in the doorway.

She held one of the large plush towels to her chest. He nodded, knowing that the sun would be rising soon. As a born vampire, Norrix had never witnessed the sun rising. Sunlight would instantly give him third degree burns. It was one of their major weaknesses.

His home, built for a vampire, was well protected against the UV rays. A special tint applied to all windows did not allow the sun to pass into the home. It was a special protective coating that was developed by vampires well over a century ago.

"Go ahead and take your time showering. I have a few calls to make," he said, backing out of the room. "You will find some clean clothes for you in the closet. They are not much, but they are something until you can get back on your feet."

"Thank you, Norrix," she said softly.

His eyes closed for a brief moment at the sound of his name on her lips.

There was no way that he could stay in the bedroom while she was naked and showering in the bathroom. He hurried from the room, shutting the door behind him.

He stalked to the kitchen, needing to get blood. He could feel his gums burning with the image of her naked body beneath the showerhead. His jeans grew tight, constricting his hardening cock.

Get a grip!

Norrix tried to will his cock to go back down, but with the sound of running water coming from the master bathroom, it had a mind of it's own.

Down, boy!

She had just been a prisoner! Sex was probably the furthest thing from her mind right now.

He snatched open the refrigerator door, finding small prepackaged bottles of blood with the blood type on the labels. He grabbed his favorite, B positive, which was chilled to perfection. Most times, he enjoyed his blood warm and straight from the donor, but now, in his overheated state, he needed something to cool off his libido.

He unscrewed the top of the blood and took a long drink. He prayed that it would help. He gums ached from his fangs wanting to descend. He grabbed his cell phone from his pocket and hit Ryan's number. Since the return of the king, vampires were slowly fitting back into the technological world. When in hiding from the human hunters, cell phones were dangerous to have. Hunters would have been able to track down

81

vampires much more easily.

"Yeah," Ryan barked into the phone.

Times were extremely stressful for the king since returning to the throne. Ryan had been overwhelmed with the daily tasks of fighting for vampires with the humans and securing their place back into society.

"It's me," Norrix answered.

"Is she settled?" Ryan's voice dropped low, as if not wanting anyone around him to hear.

Ryan was the only one that Norrix had confided in about Emely being his mate. He knew that his longtime friend would understand since he himself had just mated with the queen a few months ago.

"Almost. She's in the shower now."

"Take your time. We have everything under control at the moment," Ryan said. "Remus and Zeke are all over everything. The human leaders are still denying knowing anything of the facilities that the hunters owned."

"Well, of course they are denying any knowledge. They don't want the vampire nation to rise up and attack them as we did the hunters," Norrix growled.

"Go ahead and see to your mate," Ryan advised. "We'll discuss this when you return."

CHAPTER FOUR

~ Emely ~

The shower was almost orgasmic. It had been years since Emely had the luxury of taking a shower. She couldn't get enough of the smells of the soaps, shampoo, and conditioner. She had scrubbed her body until her skin was raw, until it was a deep, pink color. There had been so much dirt caked on her skin and in her hair. She grimaced at the color of the water that flowed down the shower drain. She was afraid to even imagine what she had looked like when Norrix and the vampire guards had rescued her and the others.

Emely stared at herself in the mirror, needing to memorize her own face again. Her gray eyes seemed overly large against her pale skin. Her dark hair, still wet from her shower, tumbled down

ARIEL MARIE

her back. She grimaced, knowing it was well past the time for a decent haircut. Her skin remained flawless, thanks to the vampiric genes she had been born with. Even through all of the experiments that the scientists had put her through, her body would heal rapidly once they would give her blood, leaving no traces of the abuse.

She untucked the towel and opened it, curious to see what her body looked like now. It had been a few years since she had been able to just look at her own body. She tried to see herself through Norrix's eyes. Every time his gaze would land on her, she could tell he wanted her. The heat that blazed from his dark eyes kept a blush on her cheeks and moisture in between her legs. Her eyes roamed over her large breasts and her dark areolas. Her nipples puckered up as the cool air gently stroked them.

Her breath caught in her throat as she imagined Norrix's large hands engulfing her mounds. Her core began to pulse as the image of his lips wrapping themselves around her hardened nipple came to mind.

Her hand slowly began to trace a path from her neck to her right aching breast. Her fingertips gently rolled her nipple before she cupped her own mound and squeezed it. Her hand continued it's own discovery of her body, sliding down her flat stomach.

She continued to imagine that it was Norrix, her savior's hands touching her, making her weak in the knees.

Her hand's slow path led to her soaked pussy. Her fingers gently dived in between her moist lips, spreading them apart as she found her sensitive nub that lay hidden away like a cherished, priceless jewel. Coated with her own juices, she gently massaged the nub, using two fingers to encircle it.

She moaned slightly, spreading her legs further so that she could properly expose herself. Her fingers continued to tease and massage her clit as moisture continued to seep out. Her fingers easily slid inside of her pussy, finding it slick and warm with need.

Locked away as a prisoner, she had been denied carnal pleasures, even from herself. Open prison cells with the constant bustle of lab employees didn't leave much for privacy.

But now, locked away in the privacy of Norrix's bathroom, she was quickly relearning the pleasures that her own hand could bring.

But this wouldn't do.

She needed more.

She paused, slowly sliding her finger out of herself. It was coated with her own wetness, but her pussy continued to pulse.

She needed him.

She craved the thought of feeling like a powerful, sexy vampire again. And the person who could help her was somewhere in the house.

She quickly wrapped the towel around herself and left out of the master suite in search of the object of her desire. She walked down the stairs and through the hallway, following the sounds of his voice. Emely knew that he had voiced the need to make a few phone calls, and found him in the kitchen with his back turned to her.

"Okay, thanks," he said into the phone, completing his call.

She dropped the towel, leaving herself exposed for him to see. His back muscles stiffened, as if he sensed that he was no longer alone in the room. Norrix turned and froze in place.

"Emely," he breathed as his eyes greedily roamed her nakedness.

"Norrix," she murmured. Without even thinking, she rushed to him with her vampire speed.

He instantly caught her in his arms and slammed his mouth against hers. It wasn't a romantic, delicate kiss. It was hard, wet, bruising, and desperate. His tongue forced its way in and she greeted it with hers, no longer shy or afraid. She needed this.

If he could find beauty in her while she looked her worst, then she knew he would be the one for her. Aside from the unexplained draw she felt the moment they first looked at each other, she knew without a doubt that destiny had brought him to her.

She wrapped her legs around his waist, needing to be closer to him. He grabbed her beneath her ass and lifted her higher, breaking the kiss. He turned and sat her down on the kitchen island. Norrix grabbed her chin and forced her to look up at him. Her eyes dropped from his and landed on his perfectly sculpted lips, catching a glimpse of his fangs.

"Are you sure," he asked, gasping for breath. Lust filled his eyes, and she could tell he was fighting to keep his control. "We don't have to do this. You don't owe me—"

"I want you," she breathed. Her fingers slowly danced down his chest, pausing at the bottom edge of his shirt. She grabbed it, and with her vampire strength, ripped the shirt from the bottom, up to the neckline.

A smile graced his lips as he shrugged off the tattered shirt. The glint in his eyes had her heart pounding away. Her eyes traced every ridge of his hardened chest, then she reached out and trailed her fingers along his muscular abdomen, fascinated as she watched them contract at her touch.

"I'm just a tad bit ticklish," he murmured, grabbing her hands and pulling her close. His warm breath caressed her neck as he trailed his sharp fangs alongside it.

She could feel the burn of her gums as her incisors broke through. She could sense the pulse of his blood flow, and the desire to bite him was strong.

Emely closed her eyes as his hands began roaming her soft flesh. She moaned as he tweaked her nipple. The roughness of his skin against hers sent a chill down her spine, causing her to spread her legs further, inviting him to her aching pussy.

His finger probed her slick lips, rubbing her clit. She gasped as he pinched her sensitive flesh—she was already so close. A few strokes and she would be there, but she had a feeling that Norrix wasn't a few strokes kind of lover.

His fingers demanded entrance to her waiting pussy. He pushed two fingers inside of her and she gripped his shoulders as he pulled them out and repeated his motion.

"You're already soaked for me," he murmured in her ear.

"Please, don't stop," she gasped, grinding her pelvis toward his hand. She squeezed her eyes tight, shivering from the sensations that overcame her as he worked her sensitive flesh.

His thumb slowly rubbed her clit, as his other fingers assaulted her aching core. Her body tensed, close to orgasm when he suddenly pulled away.

"Please," she pleaded, desperate for her first orgasm in years.

"Not allowed to come yet," Norrix murmured as he backed away, unzipping his jeans. "I want you to come on my cock."

Emely instantly missed his warmth and the feel of him stroking her. She sat back, watching as he shoved his jeans down and kicked them off. His thick cock bobbed free of his jeans. She ached to have him fill her.

Her own hand found it's way back to her pussy,

spreading her own lips open and began to rub her clit. It had been so long since she had been able to feel such pleasure, she just couldn't wait any longer.

Her breath caught in her throat as their eyes met. She continued to stroke her sensitive flesh, enjoying the sensual show she was putting on for him. He stepped back to her, not breaking eye contact. A growl escaped him as he slowly removed her hand from in between her legs.

"This belongs to me. I'll take care of her," he promised, pulling her to the edge of the counter. "Your orgasm belongs to me," he demanded, sending a chill down her spine at his dominance.

"Yes," she gasped as he lifted her up and lined up the tip of his cock to her entrance.

He slammed her down onto his cock. Emely let loose a scream of deep pleasure. Her eyes rolled into the back of her head at the feel of his wide girth stretching her. She wrapped her arms around his shoulders, holding on for dear life as he repeated the motion.

Fast and hard.

"Goddess above," she moaned around her fangs.

Norrix grunted as her pussy walls clenched around him. He wasn't delicate at all in his taking of her, and she loved every moment of it.

She crushed her mouth to his as he took a few steps, never breaking their connection. Even the taste and smell of Norrix was addictive. She would never get enough of it.

Coolness greeted Emely's back as Norrix braced the two of them against the refrigerator. She was at the edge of her euphoria with the motion of his length sliding against the inner walls of her pussy.

Each deep thrust stroked her soul. Unable to resist any longer, she tumbled head first into one of the most intense orgasms of her life. Her scream pierced the air as she broke the kiss. She gripped the hair at the nape of his neck while a flood of sensations coursed through her body.

But he was not through with her yet.

He angled her hips as he continued to thrust. She buried her head into the crook of his neck, feeling another orgasm building. His plump carotid artery pulsed as her eyes zeroed in on it. She slowly trailed her tongue along Norrix's exposed neck, tasting him, before slowly piercing his flesh with her incisors.

Norrix roared his release as she latched onto him. The rush of his thick coppery sustenance filled her mouth and slid down her throat.

There was no other way to describe the taste of Norrix. His powerful blood flowed into her, empowering her like no other had before.

After another pull, she released him and turned her neck, exposing herself to him—offering herself to him.

He pounced on Emely's exposed jugular, piercing her flesh with his fangs, laying his claim on her.

CHAPTER FIVE

~ Norrix ~

One day of lovemaking was not nearly enough for Norrix. He didn't know what pushed Emely to follow her instincts about them, but he was damn glad she did. He had anticipated having to woo her over the next few weeks, possibly even months, in order to give her time to heal from her ordeal as a captive.

They made love long into the day, finally making their way back into the master bedroom. All day long, they took their time in getting to know not only each other's bodies, but each other.

Emely, like Norrix, was a born vampire. Ten years ago, during the initial attacks of the human hunters, Emely lost her entire family. She had joined the family business, a privately owned blood bank that catered to vampires. Winter Cryo Labs had been a well-known blood dispensary for vampires to safely purchase blood. The facility was also known to compensate their human donors well.

When the humans attacked, those vampire owned blood dispensaries were the first to be destroyed. Norrix knew that while she was fighting to stay alive, he was fighting to save their people. His hatred continued to build against the human hunters as he thought back to her story, describing how she was taken captive.

She had been on her way to the Valerian mansion.

On her way to him.

Emely and many other vampires were encouraged to seek out refuge amongst their leaders. All vampire dignitaries across the country that survived offered their homes as places of safety until arrangements for safe travels to more secured locations could be made.

They could have met two years ago, but the hunters prevented his mate from coming to him.

His cell phone chirped, signaling an incoming text message. Norrix didn't want to move. He wanted to bask in the feel of having his mate lay at his side, but knew that this special moment would not last forever. He and Emely would have to return to the real world.

Emely murmured a protest in her sleep as he shifted both of their bodies so he could reach his phone. The sheet slipped, displaying Emely's naked form. He groaned internally as her dark areolas came into view. He wished that they could spend at least a week locked away together, but now would not be a good time.

The relationship between vampires and humans was rocky. Norrix would be needed by Ryan's side to secure the future of their race.

He grabbed the phone and slid his finger across the glass screen.

Meeting in thirty minutes.

The text was from Ryan. He must have news, or an assignment for him. He rubbed a hand across his face before throwing the phone back on the nightstand. He placed a small kiss to Emely's forehead.

"Where are you going?" she asked sleepily. Her hand connected with his chest, slowly sliding south.

He smiled and gripped her hand. Norrix was extremely pleased that his little mate's stamina was right there with his. But then again, to be denied sexual pleasure for two years, he would be rearing to go for at least seventy-two hours straight.

"The king is summoning me," he murmured, laying a kiss on her palm.

Emely's eyes slowly opened and Norrix swallowed hard. Her large gray pools could swallow a man whole.

"Oh," she breathed, pushing her dark hair from her face.

"But you can stay here and get your rest," Norrix said, laying another kiss on her, this time on her lips.

Emely's mouth automatically opened for him, inviting his tongue to duel with hers. The faint taste of his blood still lingered on her tongue. His cock began to harden as he deepened the kiss.

Thirty minutes was plenty of time.

Norrix pushed the blanket out of the way, rolling on top of Emely. Her legs automatically opened, allowing him to settle in between them.

"I don't have much time," he moaned, trailing kisses along her chin. Emely shifted her hips, rubbing her moist folds against the length of his cock.

"We can be quick." Emely gasped as he shifted and thrust his cock deep into her already soaked core. The tightness of her warm slick sheath wrapped around his cock had his fangs descending. "I love the feel of you in me."

"I love the way your body responds to me," Norrix groaned, brushing her hair from her face. He needed to be able to look into her eyes as he made love to her. "You're already so wet for me."

He had to pause before moving again. Norrix breathed deep, taking in the scent of Emely. He didn't know what it was about her that kept him on the edge. He shifted their position, rising up on his knees while he brought her core flush against him. The tilt of her hips gave him more leverage to thrust deeper.

"Norrix," Emely moaned. Her head pushed back into the pillows, arching her back, presenting her breasts to him.

He loved hearing his name on her lips while he brought her intense pleasure.

Emely let loose a small feminine growl as he thrust into her from the new position. Norrix was mesmerized by the sight of Emely's full breasts moving in sync with each drive of his hips. The moisture coating his dick had him increasing his pace.

Each gasp and moan from Emely increased as he pounded his length into her. He slid his hand in between them, separating her wet folds to find her swollen clit. Using his thumb, he strummed her sensitive flesh, applying slight pressure and eliciting a scream from Emely as her muscles tightened around him.

Her pussy clamped down on his cock, causing him to roar his release, shooting his seed deep into her womb. Unable to kneel any longer, Norrix's body fell forward, spent.

Emely's arms surrounded him as they lay chest to chest, neither of them able to catch their breaths. Norrix's muscles began to relax as he rested his face down on the pillow. The slight sting of Emely's fangs piercing his neck brought a slight smile to his face as his mate drank from him. He didn't mind at all. She would need her energy for later. He just couldn't get enough of her.

CHAPTER SIX

~ Norrix ~

"You're late," Ryan announced as Norrix walked into the king's office.

"My apologies," Norrix replied with a nod.

Getting to make love to Emely one more time was worth being in the hot seat with the king. He held in a groan as he thought of Emely's naked form in his bed. His cock hardened as the imagery of her supple curves came to mind. He quickly changed his line of thoughts as he walked around the table.

"I'm sure I know the reason why you are tardy, so you're excused," Ryan added with a small smile. "It wasn't too long ago that I found my mate, as you know."

"Thank you, Your Grace," Norrix said, taking a

seat at the conference table. Zeke and Remus both nodded their greeting.

Fifteen minutes late.

First time in his career that he had ever been late to work. Norrix had to fight to keep a smile off his face as the king began to speak.

"As I was saying before you came in, Norrix. Mr. Wayne, the Secretary of Defense, is determined to try to convince me that the hunters were not affiliated with their government." Ryan stood and slowly began to walk around the table.

"But yet, their government did nothing to help our entire race," Zeke growled. "We've had this discussion before. What are they going to do to fix it?"

"Supposedly, we have their full support, according to the secretary," Ryan huffed. "I sent them the report of the rescue from the first laboratory."

"We are going after the others?" Remus asked.

"Yes, without a doubt," Ryan nodded. "But, before we discuss that, I wanted to show you something."

Ryan stalked over to the computer in the corner of the room and typed in a few commands. The blank television screen mounted on the wall came to life, displaying what was left of the burned down research facility building. Remus had placed a few cameras around the property for observation after they ensured the building was destroyed.

Norrix leaned forward in his chair to focus on

the individuals on the screen. Three heavily armed human males wandered around the piles of debris scattered around where the building once stood.

"Hunters," Norrix breathed as he watched the recorded video.

"So, they were going to go back to the facility," Remus murmured, sitting back in his chair. "Shit."

"Probably to finish off the vampires that we rescued," Zeke growled, slamming his fist down on the table. "Let us go after them."

"Oh, we will," Ryan promised. "But for now, we focus on these fucking research facilities. We rescue any and all vampires that were captured, and then you are to burn the buildings to the ground, just as you did to this one."

Each vampire in the room nodded as they listened to their king. Norrix knew that this was important. In order for the king to sign the treaty with the humans, they had to ensure that all vampires were free.

"What if we hunt them down and follow them?" Norrix asked. If those fuckers were still alive, he wanted to personally find them and drain them for all the torture that Emely had went through. "They can lead us to any others that may still exist."

"I like where Norrix is going with this," Zeke agreed, rapping his knuckles on the table. "All of this love in the air, mating shit, hasn't messed with his warrior mentality."

Norrix shot Zeke a glare before turning back to the video playing. Ryan tapped a button on the keyboard, zooming in on one of the hunter's faces. Norrix made sure to memorize the scar above the right eye and black beard with a strip of gray on the chin. The human was directing his men around the grounds.

That was their leader.

Norrix would be seeing the human soon. As soon as they cleared the other research facilities, Norrix and the human hunter had a score to settle.

Norrix stood in the doorway of the home he would now share with Emely. A feeling of nostalgia came over him as he stepped into the home. It seemed as if he had waited a lifetime to be able to find that special someone to spend an eternity with. He walked through the house and found the back patio door open.

Norrix paused in the doorway, his gaze taking in the beauty of his mate in the full moonlight. Emely was stretched out on a chaise on the patio. Her head, braced with her arms behind it, was tilted back as she stared up at the darkened sky.

"Have you ever just stared up at the moon?" Her soft voice startled Norrix slightly.

He hadn't made a sound since arriving at the door, but he knew that because of their mating, they would be able to sense each other, and even speak telepathically as time moved on.

"It's been a while," he replied, stepping out of

the house. He crossed over to the patio and motioned for her to sit forward so he could slide in behind her.

Norrix enclosed Emely in his arms, and he too stared up at the full moon, trying to see it through her eyes.

"We take so much for granted," she started. "You never really know what you have until it is taken from you."

Norrix briefly squeezed her tight, wanting to lend any comfort he could to his mate. It would take her time to heal from being a captive, and he would be there with her every step of the way.

"I couldn't even begin to imagine what they did to you," he murmured in her ear. "But know this, my love. I will tear through what is left of the hunter's organization to avenge you."

Emely leaned her head back against his chest. He could smell the fresh mango from her shower gel. His cock began to stir, but he willed it back down. Now was not the time for sex.

"Before my capture, I would have been on the side of creating peace between our people and the humans," she said. Her fingers slowly caressed the back of his hand. "But after the months went by, being their lab rat—*an experiment*—I would dream of the day I'd get loose and sink my fangs into this one particular guard. I planned for the day I would kill him and the others. I ached to drain them dry for all the pain that they caused."

Norrix's breath caught in his throat at her

admission. A growl vibrated from his chest at the thought of the guard that may have harmed her.

"What guard?"

"The scientists would have the guards help with transporting us to different areas of the building for their daily trials and experiments. There was this one with a scar. He would—" Her voice broke on a sob.

She turned toward Norrix, burying her head into his chest as her shoulders shook.

The hunter's leader from the video that Ryan showed came to mind. Norrix held Emely close, running a hand down her back.

"You don't have to speak any further," he murmured, quickly devising a plan to hunt down every single hunter that was currently in hiding and kill them all. "Shhh… it's okay. They will never lay a hand on you again."

This was a promise that he would forever keep. Never again would Emely be caged like an animal. Norrix would find the worthless humans and hunt them down like the animals they were. He would take great pleasure, slowly bleeding every single one of them dry until their hearts beat no more. He would die before allowing them to take her again.

"Tell me all about the infamous Norrix Buchner." Emely's muffled voice broke through his thoughts.

He smiled down at the top of her head. Emely shifted onto her side and stared up at him. Her beautiful gray eyes were wide as she waited for him to start.

"I was born a little over one hundred years ago, in the small town of Romkove, Albania. War had spilled over into our town, and my parents being vampires wanted no part in the human war. When I was two years old, there was a new king appointed to rule Albania. It was demanded that everyone swear an allegiance to the human king. But my parents, being loyal subjects of the vampire king, Ryan's father, refused."

"What did they do?" Emely questioned, shifting slightly.

Norrix couldn't resist laying a small kiss on her forehead before continuing his story.

"They uprooted our family and moved to the United States, where the vampire king and royal family had settled. My father was hired on as a guard for the king. Ryan and I were raised together. He is one of my oldest friends."

"That's a beautiful story," she breathed. "You have followed in your father's footsteps. That is very honorable of you."

"One day, I hope my future son will continue the tradition of Buchner's guarding the king." He smiled softly at the sound of Emely's breath catching.

Family was everything to Norrix. That was a lesson instilled into him by his late father. He would do whatever he could to ensure that his family name would live on. Buchner's had always been, and would always be, protectors of the king.

CHAPTER SEVEN

~ Emely ~

Emely yawned as she finished putting the rest of her clothes on. Norrix had made arrangements for the queen to come and speak with her. She had slight butterflies in her stomach since Norrix had left earlier that evening.

The queen was coming to speak with her!

She didn't even know what to say to a queen, much less the vampire queen. She knew that she was interested in helping her get back on her feet. Her family and their business had been a well-known one before the attacks began, and would be helpful for vampires again.

She grabbed her sandals from the closet and walked barefoot toward the front of the house. She didn't want to leave the queen waiting when she arrived. According to Norrix, she should be arriving at nine o'clock that evening.

Emely glanced at the clock on the wall and noticed that she had fifteen minutes to spare.

"How do you even greet a queen?" Emely asked the empty living room as she sat on the couch to put her sandals on.

She paused after the first shoe, hearing footsteps outside on the porch.

"Of course the queen would be early," Emely whispered excitedly, jumping up from the couch. She hobbled on one foot while rushing to the door. "Great, just how I want to meet the queen—in one shoe."

She swung open the door and found the porch empty.

"That's weird," she murmured, cautiously looking around. She didn't see anything.

Warning sirens began going off in her head. She backed up quickly, pausing as a piercing pain suddenly appeared in her chest.

"What the—"

She glanced down and found a small dart protruding from her chest. She stumbled, grasping the handle of the door. She knocked the dart from her chest, but it was too late. She could already feel the affects of the dart.

"Well, look what we have here," a deep voice snapped, moving closer to her.

"You were right," another voice said. "The vampires stole our property. You're coming back with us, bitch."

Emely's eyes were losing focus. She glanced up and saw a tall, blurred figure appear on the porch as her knees gave way. Her knees stung as they slammed on to the hard wooden floors of the entryway.

Hunters.

"No," Emely whispered. She tried to crawl away from the approaching humans.

"Where do you think you're going?" the first voice snapped, grabbing hold of her leg.

"No!" Emely tried to yell, but her voice came out on a shriek. Her vision faded as she fell into a dark abyss.

What time is it? Emely thought as she fought to bring herself out of a deep fog. She remembered Norrix leaving when the sun went down. She turned to stretch and moaned slightly.

That's weird.

Their bed had a deep mattress that normally curved itself around Emely's body. Her back was on something cold, flat, and hard. Then it hit her.

The hunters.

Her eyes jerked wide open while panic settled in.

A cage.

Her body flew to a sitting position; her back slammed against the cold hard steel bars. Her breaths were rapid as she kicked the cage with her feet, trying to bust the steel door open.

She was a prisoner again.

Trapped like an animal in a cage only tall enough for her to sit up in, she knew she had to get free.

"Quit kicking the damn cage," a familiar sharp voice called out. "Filthy vampire."

Emely whimpered as she realized that it was the guard with the scar on his face. Clayton was his name, and he was the guard that took great pleasure in ensuring that she suffered at the hands of the scientists.

She unconsciously reached up and held on to the bars to keep herself from falling back over. Whatever drug that was in the dart still lingered in her system. The two human males stood at a table, looking down at a laptop, murmuring amongst themselves.

Her heart pounded against her chest as her panic increased. Emely didn't know how long she had been unconscious. She was sure Norrix was going to go crazy with worry when he realized she was gone.

Norrix would come for her.

Emely knew deep in her heart that he wouldn't rest until he had rescued her. Her heart slowed to a regular rhythm as she thought of her mate. Norrix was a strong vampire, and she knew that he would tear the humans apart for taking her again.

He had promised she would never be in a cage

again.

"Where are the others?" Clayton demanded as he walked toward her cage.

She shook her head, refusing to take her eyes off him as he drew closer to her. The other human looked up from the computer and waited for her answer.

"Not going to speak, are you?" Clayton threatened as he reached for the wand located on his belt.

She was very familiar with his tools of torture. This particular device would emit a strong electrical current. The crackling sound of the electricity filled the air.

"I don't know," Emely yelled, shifting away from him. She kept her eyes on his hand as he stood in front of the cage.

"Those vampires must have told you something," he snarled, hitting the cage with the wand.

A scream escaped from Emely as a bolt of energy surged into her body. There was no protection for her as the metal cage acted as a conductor to allow the electricity to travel into her body.

"They didn't tell me anything!" she shouted, rubbing her arms while fighting to stay in a sitting position.

"That house you were in, who owns it?" Clayton demanded.

Emely glared at the human. She refused to tell

them anything else. She didn't know where the others went, and even if she did, she wouldn't give up that information. She'd spent the past two years being tortured in ways that would make even the devil cringe. She braced herself, ready for whatever the humans had in store for her.

"There's nobody down here but you, me, and Mick," Clayton growled. "No one's in this building to hear your screams except the other prisoners down the hallway, and there's nothing they can do for you."

Emely remained silent, glaring at Clayton.

"That house she was in belongs to the vampire king's right hand man," Mick said, turning the laptop around. On the screen was a picture of Norrix's face.

Clayton bent down to Emely's level with a cynical smile on his face. Dread filled her belly as she waited to see what he would do. She didn't like the dangerous glint that appeared in his eyes.

"Damn, girl, you work fast. Free for a few seconds and you're already spreading those legs of yours," Clayton sneered. "You always were prettier than the other vampire bitches."

"Maybe she'd spread them for us, too," Mick said, moving toward her cage. Bile rose in her throat at the sight of the human grabbing his bulge. "Weren't they going to start a breeding program? See what comes of a vampire/human mating?"

"Yeah. Dr. Starr did mention that." Clayton nodded.

"Let me be the first to try her out," Mick offered, licking his lips.

Emely's grip tightened on the bars. She was willing to fight to the death before she would ever allow the guards to violate her in that way.

Please, Norrix.

Hurry.

CHAPTER EIGHT

~ Norrix ~

"The fucking humans are cocky," Remus growled, holding Norrix's arm. Norrix had just received word from his queen that Emely was not in the cottage, and there had been signs of a struggle.

The hunters had his mate.

Again.

"There is a reason for this," Zeke said, tightening his grip on Norrix. "It has to be a trap. Norrix, think! They wanted us to find them."

"They can come and get me," Norrix growled as he looked at the human establishment that he was sure held Emely.

"Zeke's right. Even though the humans said that they didn't have anything to do with the hunter's research facility, they had the addresses already waiting for us," Remus recalled. "How would they know that the king would want the addresses of these facilities? I smell a rat."

"Let. Me. Go," Norrix demanded. He didn't give a shit why the humans had the addresses on hand the minute Ryan asked for them. All he could think about right now was getting his mate out of the research facility.

The vampires had arrived a few hours before. It was a little past midnight, and they had set up camp in the woods across the street from the building where a large fence was set up around the perimeter. They had watched the humans drive a black van into an attached garage, not knowing that there was a possibility of Emely being in that van. The call from the queen had come after they had been observing the facility and finished mapping out the lay of the land.

Norrix would welcome a fight with the human hunters. He already had a score to settle with them for the first time they had kept Emely hostage, torturing and starving her.

It took both Remus and Zeke to hold Norrix back from jumping the fence and storming into the building to find his mate. He would take down any human in the building with his bare hands and bleed the fuckers dry. Norrix's fangs descended with the thought of tearing into a human's neck.

According to Summer, Emely hadn't been gone long. The queen had found fresh blood on the porch of the cottage. A blinding rage overcame

Norrix as he thought of what the bastards could have done to warrant her blood to be left behind.

"Calm the fuck down," Zeke growled. "We don't know who else is in there. We can't risk you rushing in there in a rage."

"He's right," Remus nodded. "We have to keep a level head. If you can't, then we'll go in without you."

"The hell you will," Norrix bit out around his fangs. "I am the right hand of the king."

"That was an order from your king." Ryan's voice appeared behind them. The king stormed up to them, a fierce glint in his eyes. He was dressed for battle, with weapons adorning his body.

"My King," Remus and Zeke greeted immediately, letting Norrix go in order to kneel.

Norrix held Ryan's gaze for a second before kneeling before him. They may be the best of friends, but Norrix would never show any sign of disrespect, even though he disagreed with him right now.

"You may rise," Ryan commanded. "What do we know about the humans in there," he asked, nodding toward the building.

"None of them will live past tonight," Norrix growled.

"Of that, I'm sure," Ryan responded. "What do we know about the building so far?"

It took everything Norrix had to focus on reporting what they had discovered, and the plan they originally had. They had a complete blueprint layout of the building, and each of them had already memorized it. They knew that the prisoners would be kept on the lower level, away from the sunlight.

"It looks as if the scientists aren't here this late." Remus informed Ryan. "It was just two humans in the vans, and by the looks of their shirts, they were security."

Guards.

Norrix prayed that the scarred guard that Emely had spoke of, and the one they had on the videotape, was there. Norrix would take great pleasure in killing the human guard. He deserved to die for every horrific action that he ensured Emely experienced.

"Then the time to act is now," Ryan commanded. "Suit up."

After the human developed Solaris, the vampires developed bulletproof vests that worked against the deadly bullets. Each vampire grabbed his vest from their parked trucks and got ready for their raid.

Norrix's gaze focused on the building that held his mate, and he was ready to tear through it to find her. He had promised that she would never suffer at the hands of the humans again.

And he would keep that promise.

The top floor of the building was clear. As they

quickly made their way through the building, they found plenty of evidence that the facility was currently in use, and all the employees were gone for the night.

Norrix and the others quietly infiltrated the building like a well-oiled machine. Norrix motioned to Zeke and Ryan to move to the stairwells that led to the lower levels.

He motioned to Remus for him to stay upstairs while they went below. They would need eyes on the top level since it was only the four of them. They didn't have time to wait for backup. This rescue mission needed to happen now.

Norrix held his large dagger by his side as he made his way down the stairs. The feel of the heavy weapon comforted him. With it, he would unleash his rage. Norrix had no use for human guns. With his speed and his dagger, he could easily take down a roomful of enemies. The humans holding Emely against her will deserved to feel the cold sharp end of his blade in their gut and his fangs in their necks.

The hairs on the back of his neck stood at attention at the sound of a scream echoing through the building.

Emely!

Norrix sprinted down the stairs, taking them two at a time. He tore the door open at the base of the stairs and let loose a string of curses. The door led them to a dark, empty hallway that broke off into three directions. He paused, unsure of which direction to go—left, right, or straight ahead.

Shit.

Time was of the essence, and he needed to find her *now*.

Ryan and Zeke paused behind him. Norrix strained to hear where the scream came from. His heart pounded, needing Emely to make some kind of noise to lead him in the right direction.

"Fuck, which way?" Zeke asked, keeping his voice low.

"Norrix, you go that way—" Ryan was suddenly cut off by the sound of a large crash from the left. Norrix immediately took off toward the crash, with Ryan and Zeke close behind him. He followed the sounds of a struggle, followed by cursing, behind a set of double doors.

Norrix didn't hesitate as he crashed into the doors with his shoulder and came to an abrupt halt in the doorway. Rage consumed him at the sight of the two human males struggling with Emely.

They had her pinned down on an exam table, half naked.

Red clouded his vision.

These humans must die.

CHAPTER NINE

~ Emely ~

Clayton and Mick had managed to wrestle her out of her cage and stripped her of her pants. She had fought them the whole way, and even received a couple of punches to the face as they tried to subdue her. She refused to go quietly. They would have to kill her to get what they wanted. It took both of them to slam her down on the exam table. Clayton had strapped her chest down, while Mick had worked on securing one of her legs.

The door burst open, and there stood one pissed off vampire with one menacing looking dagger in his hand.

"Norrix!" Emely screamed at the site of her mate standing at the door.

Norrix in full-blown battle mode was a force to

be reckoned with. One look at her, his eyes darkened and his lip curled, displaying his massive fangs.

"Vampire—" Clayton's voice was cut off as Norrix's body crashed into his.

The screams of the human echoed through the room as Norrix took out his revenge on the human guard.

Mick tried to run from the room, but was stopped by two more massive vampires blocking the exit to the room. Emely gasped, recognizing the vampire king with the other vampires.

"Where do you think you're going," the other vampire guard growled, snatching Mick up by the throat. Mick released a tortured scream as the other vampire impaled him with a short sword.

"Are you okay?" the king asked, appearing at her side. He grabbed a sheet from underneath the table and covered her.

"Yes, Your Grace," she said, her eyes searching for Norrix.

Her mate rose from the floor, covered in blood. She knew without a doubt that Clayton was dead. She didn't need to ask. The blood covering him was proof enough. Their eyes met and he rushed to her side, assisting the king in releasing her from her restraints.

"Did they hurt you?" Norrix asked, his eyes filled with guilt.

His fingertips brushed the aching side of her face where she was sure a bruise was forming from

Clayton's punch. Her head instinctively turned to him, needing to feel his touch.

"No," she whispered as her eyes filled with tears. She blinked a few times. "Nothing I couldn't handle."

Norrix had promised that he would tear the humans apart, and from the looks of the mutilated bodies laying on the floor, he had kept his word.

"Let's get you home," he murmured, gathering her in his arms and wrapping the blanket around her.

"Wait," she said as they walked out of the room. She'd remembered what Clayton had bragged about. Norrix paused and looked down at her. "There are more. Clayton said that the others wouldn't be able to help me. There are other prisoners here."

Norrix looked to the king and the other vampires.

"Get your mate to safety," the king said, patting Norrix on the shoulder. "We'll handle the rest."

EPILOGUE

~ Emely ~

Two weeks had passed since Norrix had rescued Emely for the second time. He was her knight in shining armor. Her rescuer. Her lover. Her mate.

And she was totally in love with him.

Norrix had spent the last two weeks showing her how much he loved her. Her body was deliciously sore in certain areas, and she had no regrets about it at all.

Since her latest rescue, Norrix had been working tirelessly beside the king in helping the vampires that were rescued the night Clayton had taken her. Twelve vampires had been entrapped in that building. There was one more facility for them to check out and ensure that no vampires were being imprisoned before the king would sign the treaty with the human government.

Even Emely had volunteered to help in the infirmary. She refused to sit at home, knowing that there were others like her that were in need. She couldn't offer much, except to sit and talk with some of the vampires. Emely had a clear understanding of what they had experienced and found that it helped not only them, but her, as well. The royal physicians may be able to heal their flesh wounds, but it would take some time for them to heal mentally.

She smiled as she walked into the royal gardens with Norrix by her side. She was finally going to have the meeting with the queen that she was supposed to have the night Clayton had kidnapped her.

"The gardens are so beautiful," she gasped, looking around. The area was highlighted with small lights that lined the walkway. "And so romantic. How can anyone think of anything but romance, and being with the one they love?"

"That was the object of the gardens when Ryan's mother designed them," Norrix said, drawing her body closer to his muscular one. "She wanted to have a peaceful place to share that was full of beauty and the wonders of nature."

"It's breathtaking," she murmured.

She breathed in the scent of Norrix as she leaned into him and continued to stroll to the meeting place.

"Here they are," Norrix said as they came to an

opening with a few benches and a pond. The royal couple stood from where they sat. A few guards were posted around the area, ensuring that they were protected.

"You're Graces," Emely greeted them.

"Oh, please. Call me Summer. It is an honor to meet Norrix's mate," Summer said with a smile, grabbing Emely into a tight hug.

"Um...okay." Emely returned the queen's hug. "Thank you."

"Please, have a seat." Summer motioned to the edge of the pond, while Norrix and Ryan sat on the bench across from them. "I'm sure you are wondering why I wanted to meet with you."

"A little," Emely admitted.

She groaned internally, knowing that she had just lied to the queen. She had been a ball of nerves with the thought that the queen wanted to meet with her. Norrix had assured her repeatedly that the meeting would be fine.

"Well, don't be." The queen smiled and grabbed Emely's hand. "This is very simple, and something that you are well-aware of that our people need."

"Oh?" Emely's eyes met Norrix for a brief second before returning to Summer's. "And what is that."

"We want to help you get back onto your feet."

"You do?" Emely's heart raced at the thought of regaining her life and starting over.

"Yes, we do," Ryan said. "You're family has provided a service to vampires across this country for centuries, and we want you to bring it back."

"Winter Cryo Labs is needed again," Summer continued where Ryan left off. "What do you say?"

Emely turned to Norrix and found love shining in his eyes. She knew that he would be there for her, always. Destiny led him to rescue her from that prison cell. It was time for her to take back her life and move forward with her mate by her side.

She owed it to her family and vampires everywhere to reopen her family's blood bank. Rebuilding the family's empire would show vampires everywhere that it was time to force their way back into society. She would honor her family's legacy, and they would always be remembered for their hard work in providing safe blood to vampires everywhere.

There was no doubt in her mind that she would start over, only this time, she would have her mate at her side.

"Absolutely. Winter Cryo Labs will re-open."

~The End~

ILENA'S DESTINY

AN EROTIC VAMPIRE SERIES, VOL. 3

CHAPTER ONE

~ Ilena ~

The busy hallway of the royal mansion was astounding. She had to duck and dodge many servants and workers as she followed the head servant to the queen, Lucilla. Ilena Otoño was ecstatic that she had finally made it to the mansion, having heard that displaced vampires were welcome there. The king and queen were offering assistance for vampires who had lost everything and needed to start over.

"Is your suite to your liking?" Lucilla asked, as Ilena caught up to walk beside her down the long hallway.

"Oh, yes. It's much better than what I had grown accustomed to," Ilena replied with a nod.

She cringed on the inside with the thoughts of

where she had been sleeping over the past ten years, since the hunters began trying to decimate the vampire race. Ever since the first attacks, she had been on the run, moving every six to nine months, living in fear that she would be killed just because she was a vampire.

Many of her family didn't make it. She'd heard of a few cousins here and there that had survived, but since all surviving vampires had went off the grid in order to survive, communication around the world was difficult. Many electronic devices that humans took for granted, vampires had to avoid for fear of being tracked down. Cell phones, tablets, and laptops had trackers, and vampires knew they couldn't own one, not if they wanted to stay alive.

The vampires had been at the top of the food chain until the human hunters decided that they didn't like sharing the planet with supernatural beings. Life had been peaceful before the attacks, but a certain special interest group of humans began a war on the vampires that they were ill-prepared for.

"Okay, here we are," Lucilla said as she paused beside a doorway. "The royal nurses will be a great fit for you."

"I'm nervous," Ilena admitted, brushing her hands against the front of her jeans. Her heart sped up at the thought of working as a nurse again. "It's been so long since I've even practiced. What if I forgot everything I learned in school, or picked up during my career?"

"You'll be fine." Lucilla grabbed her shoulders and pulled Ilena to face her. Her warm smile and friendly eyes caused Ilena to relax slightly. "They will help ease you back into the field of nursing. Every single one of them has been in your shoes. You are amongst your people now."

Her people.

Tears blurred her vision as she smiled. It was like a weight had been lifted off her shoulders at hearing such kind words. She barked a quick laugh as she brushed the tears from her cheeks.

"I'm sorry," she laughed.

"Oh, don't be sorry. You've been through so much." Lucilla leaned in and grabbed Ilena in a strong embrace. Ilena returned the hug, feeling comforted by the fellow vampire.

"Thank you. I guess I needed to hear that," she admitted, pulling back.

"No problem. Now, dust yourself off. Through these doors, your future awaits you."

The past two weeks had been wonderful. Getting back into the nursing field was, as the humans would say, like riding a bike.

Loud voices filled the hallway, drawing Ilena's attention. She glanced toward the door before turning back to her small patient. A vampire girl, who had burned her hand, was brought to the infirmary by her concerned mother.

"Keep it wrapped. I believe it's only second-degree burns. Air will cause it to sting," she instructed the young girl's mother. She finished putting the tape around the gauze dressing, and couldn't help but smile at the little vampire.

"Thank you, Nurse Ilena," the woman said.

"It's my pleasure," Ilena replied, pride filling her chest. "You are so brave, little one. Now, remember, fire in a fireplace is not a toy," she gently scolded the little girl with a small smile.

"Yes, ma'am," she whispered, as pain showed in her bright eyes.

"The pain salve should kick in shortly and ease your pain, little one. I'll also give you some to take with you." Ilona assisted the little girl down from the exam table. Once assured that she was safely with her mother, Ilena grabbed the bag of dressing supplies and pain salve she had prepared.

"I can't thank you enough," the mother said. They both jumped as loud shouting increased outside the exam room's door.

"What in the world?" Ilena muttered, stepping over to the door. She opened it to find two large vampires rushing past, carrying another one in their arms, headed into the larger bay area of the infirmary. She could hear Dr. Cain shouting orders to the other royal nurses.

"Be careful on your way out," Ilena advised as she guided the young mother and child in the right direction, out of the large infirmary. She glanced up and her eyes widened at the figures that were stalking down the hallway, in the direction the other vampires had just went.

It's King Ryan, and the leader of the royal guard, Norrix!

She instantly stepped to the side and lowered her head out of respect as they passed her. She was in complete awe of the king. Legendary stories were already being told of his magnificent return last year.

She had prayed, along with many vampires, for his return. She knew deep down that he didn't die all those years ago, when the royal mansion was attacked. She'd had faith that he would return and save vampires everywhere. In the past year, since his return, things had already begun to look up for vampires.

Her eyes lifted and she watched as they entered the main sick bay.

What was going on?

Curiosity got the best of her, and she found herself following in their wake. She stopped at the entryway and paused. Dr. Cain and other nurses were scrambling around an injured vampire that laid on the cot in the center of the infirmary. Ilena could tell that he was one of the royal guards by the tactical uniform that he wore, which matched King Ryan's and Norrix's.

She watched, fascinated, as the head royal nurse, Bernia, cut the tattered shirt from the patient's muscular body. Her heart fluttered as his well-defined arms were now on display as Bernia moved around to the other side of the cot. Her eyes widened even further at the direction her thoughts were headed.

This vampire was quite possibly lying on his deathbed, and she was busy admiring his muscular arms. No matter how fine of a specimen he was, she should never have those thoughts for a patient.

"Ilena!" Bernia's voice caused her to jump as her attention flew to the head nurse.

"Yes, ma'am?"

"Come help. We could use another set of hands," Bernia said, motioning for her.

Ilena's eyes looked to the king and his guards as she moved across the room. They stood back, out of the way, and let the medical personnel work on their fallen brother. Ilena's feet carried her to the side of the bed, where she began to work with Bernia to disrobe the unconscious vampire.

Her heart raced as she finished removing his pants. Sweat began to form as she tried to be professional and not look to see what God had given him in-between his legs, but she failed. Her eyes quickly glanced at the bulge that was beneath his cotton boxer briefs.

Her hands trembled as she moved to wash the blood from his legs. What was wrong with her? She was becoming slightly aroused by an unconscious vampire!

Who was this man? she wondered.

She shook her head and refocused on the task at hand. She needed to cleanse his wounds properly to prevent infection. Vampires were immortal and their bodies could heal on their own, but there was nothing like a bad infection to delay healing time.

Dr. Cain and Bernia worked from the other side of the cot and continued to assess the patient. The other nurses scurried off to bring in the portable scanner as Dr. Cain had ordered.

"What's your prognosis of Remus?" The king's voice broke through the silence.

Ilena moved on autopilot as her skills as a nurse came forth. She gathered the supplies she would need and came back to the vampire's side. A couple weeks ago, she had been afraid that she'd forgotten everything, but once in action, everything came back to her.

"His body should heal on its own. The body armor that your men wear protected his vital organs from the shrapnel. Now we just have to wait for his brain to heal. Even in vampires, brain injuries can be tricky," Dr. Cain informed the king as he moved to stand by him.

Ilena's eyes traveled up the length of the warrior and she swallowed hard. Even under all the grime and dirt, she could see he was a fine specimen of a vampire. Moisture began to gather at her center as she began to imagine what he would look like thrusting into her.

Stop! She mentally yelled at herself. What was wrong with her? There were people in the room and here she was, practically drooling over this warrior. Her hands began to tremble again as she took up cleaning his wounds.

"Thank you, Dr. Cain," the king said. "Please, keep me updated on his recovery."

"Of course, Your Grace. Remus will receive the best care that we can offer," Dr. Cain assured him. "We shall have around the clock care for him, and arrange for a nurse to stay with him twenty-four seven until he wakes."

Ilena kept working as the physician spoke to the king and other warriors. She worked her way up to his chest, while trying to keep all inappropriate thoughts from her mind.

"Ilena, I'll start the transfusion." Bernia appeared at Ilena's side with a bag of blood. The blood transfusion would help the vampire's body to heal more quickly. A vampire's sole means of nutrition came from all the protein and nutrients found in blood. "You've adapted well since arriving here at the mansion."

"Thank you." Ilena could feel her cheeks warm at the praise of the head nurse. She taped the dressing to his pectoral muscle, where the wound was already starting to heal right before her eyes.

"That's why I'm assigning you to watch over this warrior."

CHAPTER TWO

~ Remus ~

The building was dark as night. Remus cursed under his breath as he and Zeke crept through the silent building in tandem. Their king had dispatched them to another research facility in search of other captured vampires. The untrustworthy humans had lied before, and this time, the king was not taking any chances of leaving any vampires behind.

Their mission was easy.

The addresses to each known facility had been handed over by the human government, and the vampires were to ensure that indeed all vampires had been freed.

Remus crept down the hallway with his weapon drawn, Zeke close behind. He came upon a door and motioned for Zeke to halt. They worked together like a well-oiled machine, and he knew that he could trust Zeke to have his back. His ears perked up when he heard what sounded like someone singing. The voice was beautiful. He paused and leaned near the door, the voice getting louder.

Who would be singing? It must be a captive, trying to find a way to console themselves while being a tortured subject for the human scientists.

He turned and found Zeke no longer behind him. He frantically looked down the hallway in search of him, but there was no trace of him.

What the fuck?

Where in the hell did he go? He glanced around, and the building slowly faded away before his eyes. He blinked in disbelief and swung his now empty hand up, as if to aim a weapon that was no longer there. He found himself in a hallway that went on for miles each way. He looked back at the door and saw a glowing light coming from beneath it.

What the hell was going on?

The feminine voice grew stronger. It was angelic, and a feeling he had never felt before washed over his soul. He braced his hands on the doorjamb and closed his eyes, loving the sound of whoever it was singing. He twisted the knob to the door, and it gave way with a slight click. His heart rate increased. He had to find the person with the sweet voice.

The door slowly opened on its own, and the bright light blinded him. He cringed and covered his eyes, unable to withstand the brightness. He jumped back, anticipating the sensation of burning flesh from the sun, but it never came.

He lowered his arms in confusion and squinted, trying to see what was in the room.

"Remus?" A voice called his name from the bright light. He paused before deciding to head toward the source. He didn't know why, but he had to follow the voice. He slowly stepped into the room.

"Remus. Can you hear me?" the voice asked.

"Yes," he murmured. "Where are you?" He looked around as the light slowly dimmed, until he was left in complete darkness.

"Open your eyes, honey," the voice instructed.

"Remus, squeeze my hand," the angelic voice instructed.

He let loose a groan, the pounding pain in his head causing him to wince. A small hand slipped into his. It was much smaller than his, and the softness of it was in direct contrast to the calluses on his. He didn't understand why, but he knew he didn't want to hurt his angel, so he squeezed it, gently.

"Can you open your eyes?" she asked.

"Yes." His voice cracked as he answered. He swallowed a few times, and had to work to get his tongue off the roof of his mouth. He reached up with his free hand to rub his face, and practically had to pry his eyes open. He blinked a few times to adjust to the light in the room.

"There you are." He could hear the smile in her

voice, and turned to finally see who his angel was. He was rendered speechless.

Her bright eyes gazed upon him curiously. Her smile captivated him, and deep down, he knew that he wanted to see her smile more and be the reason that she did. He could tell by the look in her eyes that her smile was a rare one. He knew that life for a vampire hadn't been easy over the past eleven years.

"Here, let me get you something to drink." Getting up from the bedside chair, she walked to the other side of the room. He was completely mesmerized by the sound of her voice, which had a slight hint of a Spanish accent.

Remus flexed his hand, instantly missing the warmth from her small one. His eyes remained locked on her curvy frame as she bustled around on the other side of the room.

Her chocolate eyes returned his gaze as she made it back to his side. He made a move to sit up, but winced as the pounding in his head resumed.

"Be careful," she exclaimed, sitting the small glass down on the side table. "Let me help you."

He waved her off. She was much smaller than him, and she wouldn't be able to successfully move him up in the bed alone.

"I can do it." He grimaced as he slowly inched his way up to lean against the backboard. He would never show such weakness in front of a female. Remus Vorigan was a royal guard for the king, dammit! He could do something as simple as sit up in a damn bed. But after finishing the task, he realized how weak he had become, and had to fight to control his breathing.

"Here." She offered him the small goblet, and the delicious smell of fresh warm blood reached his nostrils. He took the cup from her, noting the little bolt of electricity that shot through his arm at the touch of her fingertips to his. Tipping the cup back, he attempted to drink his fill, but ended up sputtering as it went down the wrong pipe.

"Slow down." She laughed as she placed a hand on his, and pushed the cup away from his mouth. He coughed a few times in an attempt to clear his throat. He didn't know how long he had been unconscious, but however long it was, it was just too damn long to go without sustenance.

"Who are you?" he asked once he was able to breathe again. He slowly raised the cup to his lips again, and this time, sipped from the goblet.

"I'm Ilena. I work with the royal nurses," she stated, tucking a strand of loose hair behind her ear. His eyes tracked her every move. He paid particular attention to the color warming her cheeks that he wanted to examine closer.

"I've never seen you before. I would remember you if I had." He searched through his memory and knew that if he had seen her, he definitely would have remembered her. She had a face that he knew he would never forget, and her body screamed sexy, with curves in all the right places.

No, they had never met before.

"I just arrived about two weeks ago," she said as he finished off the blood. It wasn't straight from the host, but it would do. The leader of the royal guard, Norrix's mate, Emely, was rebuilding her family's laboratory that would enable humans to voluntarily donate their blood for vampires. With her work, the supplies of bagged blood had increased.

"What was that song you were singing to me?" he asked, breaking the comfortable silence. She took the empty goblet from him and stood. "That was you I heard singing, right?"

"It's just a silly song *mi abuela* taught me when I was a little girl," she answered, shyly.

His hand shot out and grabbed her arm as she went to move away. Ilena's shocked gaze met his before trailing down to where his hand encircled her wrist. His eyes followed hers, and he gazed upon where their skin met. His thumb slowly traced circles on her soft brown skin. His heart sped up as the image of their naked bodies entangled together came to mind.

He wanted her.

"It was beautiful. You have the voice of an angel," he said honestly. If it hadn't been for her singing, he may have still been trapped in the nightmare he thought had been real.

"Thank you," she murmured. He watched her eyes, and he would have sworn a hint of desire shot through them before disappearing.

Did she feel it too?

"I need to call the doctor and the king to alert them that you're awake."

CHAPTER THREE

~ Ilena ~

Ilena stood outside while the physician and the king spoke to Remus alone. She leaned her head back against the wall and breathed deeply. She thought that the vampire guard was handsome while he was unconscious, but now, awake, he was dangerously wicked. His intense eyes didn't leave her once while she was in the room.

The feel of his calloused hands on her soft wrist had her wanting to tear her clothes off and jump on him, to feel the roughness of his naked body against hers. But she had to control herself. Using the excuse of calling the physician and the king was more for her sake than his.

She was a refugee, making a home at the king's mansion, and was now able to work again as a healer, a nurse for her people. She couldn't mess this up over her infatuation with her patient.

A king's guard at that!

Daytime was approaching, and she could feel the weariness in her body start to set in. Vampires were nocturnal by nature, never able to enter the world during the daytime, for they all inherited a severe allergy to the sun. The rays would burn their flesh, and even burn them alive.

She jumped at the sound of the door opening. Dr. Cain exited the room and paused next to her.

"I'm giving him one more day of rest in bed. By tomorrow, he should be back to his normal self," he said, tossing his physician's bag over his shoulder.

"Yes, Doctor." She nodded, standing a little straighter.

"I want you to stay with him, see to his needs, and call me if his headache persists."

"Of course, Dr. Cain. Thank you." He patted her on the shoulder as he walked off.

Spend another day with her sexy as sin patient? God help her. She moved to stand by the door and found the king helping Remus from the bathroom.

"Your Grace! I can do that!" She rushed into the room, arriving at the other side of Remus. She wrapped an arm around his waist and helped guide him. She internally groaned at the feel of his muscular back beneath her arm.

"It's fine," Ryan chuckled as they arrived at the bed. "He was just a little unsteady on his feet, and I didn't want one of my best guards falling face-first on the ground at my feet."

"I'm not that weak," Remus scoffed, sitting down on the edge of the bed. "It was a slight trip, and both of you are fretting over me like I'm handicapped. You heard Dr. Cain, I'll be back to normal by nightfall."

"Well, see that you are," Ryan said before walking to the door, where he paused. "Nightfall, our job continues. Get some rest."

Ilena watched as the king shut the door, leaving her alone again with Remus. She turned to him and swallowed hard. This hardened warrior, dressed only in sleeping pants, showcasing every hardened ridge of his chest and abdomen, sat on the bed with his intense eyes locked on her.

Flashbacks of her bathing him, to get all the blood and dirt off came to her mind. Her hands shook with the knowledge of what those ridges felt like beneath her hands. She craved to know how he would feel against her, naked. Her eyes trailed up his body to meet his. How was she going to spend an entire day with him?

"What are you thinking about?" Remus's deep voice broke through her inappropriate thoughts.

"There are some things better left unknown," she whispered, unable to look away from him. Her heart began to pound as the color of his eyes deepened.

"There are some things better left to be discovered," he murmured. Gently grabbing her wrist, he pulled her closer to him until she stood between his legs. His hands rested on the back of her thighs, and every conscious thought went out the window. "Your body gives off small signs of what's running through that brain of yours. I can tell right now that you want me, just as much as I want you, to be buried deep inside of you."

Her breath caught in her throat at his words. She was unable to resist this draw to him, and the look in his eyes revealed that he felt the same. Moisture collected at her core with the heat pouring from his eyes. Her hands moved on their own and gently cupped his rugged jawline as she leaned in and covered his mouth with hers.

The kiss, soft at first, grew harder as the urgency to feel every inch of his hardened body against hers grew. Remus immediately took control of the kiss as his tongue invaded her mouth. He crushed her body to his, her nipples now sensitive, even through her scrub shirt. She needed to feel his hands on her naked flesh.

She broke the kiss and quickly pulled her shirt over her head. His hands reached up and unhooked the front clasp of her bra, freeing her aching mounds. She let loose a moan as he took one of her breasts into his hot mouth, drawing it in deep as he pinched and squeezed the other. She threw her head back in ecstasy as he nipped at her sensitive nipple, before soothing it with his tongue.

His hands pushed her scrub pants down and took her panties with them. She kicked off her shoes, then pants, leaving her naked for him to see.

"Perfection," he murmured as his eyes took all of her in. She relaxed as the slight insecure feelings of carrying extra pounds dissipated under his heated gaze, which lingered on her sex.

He slid a single finger in-between her plump folds, eliciting a gasp from her. She grabbed onto his shoulders as his finger dove deeper into her slickness. She closed her eyes and bit her lip to keep from crying out as his finger continued to move, spreading her wetness to her clit. Her legs shook as he found her hidden nub and began to apply pressure to it.

Remus braced his free hand on her hip as he continued to work her clit. Her hips moved in sync with his finger as he quickened his pace. She opened her eyes, finding his gaze locked on her as he continued.

"Remus," she moaned out his name, unable to form any other conscious thought. Her core pulsated, demanding to be filled by him. She needed to feel his thick cock deep inside of her. "Please," she begged as the tension began to build in her body from his talented finger.

"Not yet," he answered, nipping her breast with his fangs. He sucked her mound deep into his hungry mouth, while he continued his assault on her pussy. Her hands threaded their way into his hair as she hung on for dear life.

"Oh my—" she gasped as he added a second finger. Her gums ached and burned as her fangs descended. Ilena's muscles began to tighten as she gripped his hair harder, as she continued to ride his hand. "Remus."

This time, his name was dragged out of her as she threw her head back from the intensity. The sensation of his mouth around her nipple and fingers playing with her slick, swollen nub was getting to be too much for her.

"Yes," he murmured against her aching breast. "Now you can come," he instructed, pinching her clit.

Her body, no longer under her control, drew tight and jerked forward as the waves of her orgasm flooded her. She buried her head into the crook of his neck as her body shuddered uncontrollably. The tension in her muscles slowly faded, leaving her in an utterly relaxed state.

"Oh, my," she whispered against his neck. Her arms were like lead, wrapped around Remus's neck. She didn't think she could even move.

"Hang on." She felt him shift his body and grabbed her by the back of her legs, lifting her up.

She felt the head of his cock at the entrance of her still pulsating core. She shifted her hips and dropped down onto him, taking all of him at once, causing him to shout. She let loose a silent scream into his neck as her pussy burned from being stretched so wide. She breathed deep, taking in the slight hint of his musk, with a slight hint of soap. His hands gripped the plump meat of her ass as she began to move her hips, lifting up before sliding back down on his thickness.

"Yes," she hissed, no longer able to control herself. His artery pulsed beneath the skin of his neck, alerting her to the flow of his blood. She was tempted.

Bite him. Claim him, a voice whispered into the back of her mind.

"Fuck," Remus growled as she continued to take his entire length deep into her slick core. His grip tightened on her ass as he slammed her down onto his cock. Her pussy clenched from the deep invasion, and her body began to tremble as she continued to ride him. Emotions that began to swell into her chest were from somewhere deep within her.

"*Tú me perteneces,*" she whispered against his neck, unconsciously. *You belong to me.*

She knew she would never be able to leave this vampire. Somehow, she knew that he was hers, so she threw caution to the wind and sunk her fangs deep into his plump artery.

CHAPTER FOUR

~ Remus ~

Remus growled at the sharp pierce of Ilena's fangs into his flesh. His balls drew tight as he continued to slam into Ilena's tight sheath. He was out of control. He wanted to possess her, body and soul. He would never give up this little vampire nurse.

Everything was perfect about her, right down to the way her pussy gripped him. Unable to hold back any longer, Remus gripped her tight to him, leaving him sheathed within her slick pussy as he released inside of her. A shudder racked through his body and he growled again as her tight walls clenched around him, continuing to milk him. Ilena released his neck and sealed the wound with her tongue.

He grabbed the back of her head and leaned his

forehead against hers, trying to catch his breath. He wasn't sure what the words were that she whispered in her native tongue, but he was sure that she had just laid claim to him. He searched within himself and found that he loved it.

Claim her, a voice whispered in the back of his mind. His limp cock began to stir again as she shifted her hips. He held back an internal groan at the feel of her still slick pussy gripping his hardening cock.

"I'm not sorry," she whispered, out of breath.

"Don't be," he replied, pulling her head back. He needed to see her eyes. He wanted to be able to see the true feelings there. "What did you say?"

She opened her eyes, and he could see the slight hint of hesitation before she spoke. "You belong to me," she whispered.

"I'm honored." His fingers drifted along her jawline and sunk into her thick, dark hair.

His eyes trailed down to her swollen lips and he knew, deep down, that he loved the idea. His little vixen knew what she wanted, and didn't hesitate in laying her claim on him. The action alone was just downright sexy.

"I'll understand if you—"

He gripped her hair and gently pulled her head back again, exposing her neck to him, causing her words to fade off. Her lips parted in anticipation as he trailed his tongue along her neck, tasting the slight saltiness of her skin. His gums burned as his fangs broke through. He would never have her thinking that he didn't want her in return. He believed in love at first sight. Look at what happened with Ryan and Norrix with their mates.

Instant attraction.

Destiny.

Vampires had been through so much the last decade that he wouldn't miss out on the opportunity that was being presented to him. There was a reason she came to the royal mansion.

Destiny led her to him.

He decided to torture his little vixen a little by trailing his fangs against her skin. His attempt to torture her backfired on him, though. Her wiggling on his lap caused his hardened cock to swell even more.

"You belong to me," he whispered before sinking his fangs into her jugular.

"Congratulations," Ryan said, standing from behind his desk to offer his hand. Remus shook his king's hand, pride filling his chest. He had just announced to the room that he had found his destined mate. He was meeting with Ryan, Norrix, and Zeke in Ryan's office to discuss what had went wrong at the human's laboratory. Since the accident, they hadn't had a chance for a full debriefing with the king.

A few months ago, the vampires discovered at a meeting with the human leaders about these facilities. The king demanded the locations of them all so that they could be decommissioned. It was at one of the facilities that Norrix's mate, Emely, had been discovered, along with a group of other captured vampires. It was there the human scientists tortured the hostages, and sometimes killed them in the name of science and research.

Zeke groaned from his chair with a roll of his eyes. Norrix balled up a piece of paper and tossed it at him.

"Ignore him," Norrix said, standing and pulling him in for a manly hug. "He's just jealous because there's no one out there for him."

"I don't want just one person for all eternity. I'd rather have my pick when I get an itch," Zeke snapped, a scowl spreading across his face. "All this love in the air crap is for romance books."

"Zeke," Ryan warned.

"It's fine," Remus said. He knew that his friend was against settling down with one person. His attitude had been the same when Ryan had mated with Summer, and Norrix with Emely. Zeke had never shown any disrespect to Summer or Emely, but he didn't bite his tongue when he was with the men.

"We need to talk about what happened," Ryan began, speaking of the night Remus was nearly blown to bits.

"We made it into the building without any issues," Zeke informed the room, once everyone was settled in their chairs. "Same as the other ones.

It appeared abandoned, but we knew to move through it with extreme caution."

Remus nodded in agreement as Zeke continued to inform Ryan of what happened. It was a small building, and they hadn't thought anyone was inside. Zeke and Remus, being dispatched to get intel, used a heat sensor on the building in an attempt to detect anyone, human or vampire. They had radioed in to Ryan and Norrix, informing them that the technology didn't pick up on any bodies inside the building. After a brief discussion, it was decided that the plan would change from gathering intel, to investigating if it was cleared as the humans promised, and destroy it.

"We entered into the basement to ensure that it was clear since the heat sensor's reach didn't extend to the basement," Remus said, taking over the story. Memories of that night flashed before his eyes. If only he would've listened to his gut once they had reached the bottom step. "It was a trap."

"Remus is right. The minute we stepped off the last stair, everything went straight to hell," Zeke added.

Remus recalled that when they had reached the lower-level of the building, one of them tripped a wire. A series of clicks had them running up the stairs, but it was too late. The building shook as it was blown to pieces. Remus didn't have any recollection once the building exploded. He owed Zeke his life. If it hadn't been for his friend pulling him out of the collapsing building, he certainly would have perished. His body was banged up pretty bad. Thankfully, being a vampire saved his life. Had he been human, he would have died that night.

"Were there any vampires in the building?" Remus had to know. Did they fail at saving more of their people?

"No." Ryan shook his head. "We went back the following day at dusk with a team and went through the rubble. There were no bodies found."

"Do we know who rigged the building?" Remus asked, clenching his fists. At least the building was cleared. He ached to strangle whoever almost took their lives.

"We're looking into it now." Ryan tapped his fingers on the table. "Someone will pay for this."

Murmurs of agreement echoed around the room.

"So what's next?" Remus questioned, sitting forward. He was ready to finish what they had started. It was imperative that vampires could feel safe again. Their king had finally returned, which was what they all had so desperately needed. There was one more building that needed to be swept and destroyed. Once that was done, Ryan would finish the negotiations with the human leaders.

"Nothing for you today." Ryan smiled. "Go help your mate get settled into your quarters. The sun will be rising soon. That goes for all of you. Rest. Tonight, we hunt."

CHAPTER FIVE

~ Ilena ~

Excitement bubbled inside of Ilena as she stared around at Remus's living quarters—*their* living quarters. She sat her small bag of belongings on the small couch before walking into his bedroom. She finally had a place to call her own. She glanced around and noted the plain decor, but she was more than okay with it. Next, she entered the bathroom.

She grinned at the thought of a private shower. She would no longer have to share a public bathroom. Her old room situation in the mansion had her sharing a common bathroom like a college dormitory.

Her life since the first attacks hadn't been pleasant, and it was much more than she was used to. Over time, she was sure she would add her personal touches to the quarters to make it homier for her and her mate.

Her mate.

She couldn't believe that she was now a mated vampire. She knew that she took a huge risk. What if he had denied her? She would have been humiliated. But for him to immediately reciprocate the gesture let her know that it was meant for them to find each other.

Destiny.

She smiled as she twirled around, but drew to a halt, finding the subject of her thoughts leaning against the door, quietly watching her with a small smile on his lips.

"Hi," she said, her feet frozen in place.

Her eyes greedily took all of him in. His broad shoulders, intense eyes, and dark hair had moisture gathering at the apex of her thighs. She swallowed hard. After the intense lovemaking and mating, one would think that they would both be satisfied.

She craved Remus. She didn't think she would ever get enough of him. One look from him and she was ready to tear her clothes off again.

"Hello yourself," he chuckled. "I thought you would be down at the infirmary."

"Apparently, the royal couple ordered me to take the day off," she murmured, unable to look away from his intense eyes.

She'd been surprised when she reported to work and the head nurse had informed her that she'd been ordered to go spend the day with her mate. Her mouth had hit the ground when she was told that it was a direct order from the king.

"Seems it was meant for us to spend the day together," he surmised, stepping into the room. "I was sent home too."

"What did you have in mind?" she asked, tilting her head back to meet his gaze as he came to a halt in front of her.

"I was thinking that since you already bathed me when I was unconscious, I could return the favor."

"Really?" Her voice ended on a squeak.

"Yes, really," he answered with a sexy smirk.

She was unsure of what to do as he opened the shower door and flipped the handles, turning the water on. She was unable to move as she watched him peel his shirt over his shoulders and toss it to the floor. She gulped.

He was perfect.

His perfectly sculpted pectoral muscles rippled as he shoved his jeans down and kicked them off, leaving him in just his boxer briefs.

"You just going to stand there? Or do you need help?" His fangs peeked from beneath his lip as he smiled at her.

Her brain finally decided to kick in, allowing her to move. She pulled her scrub top over her head and gasped, finding him directly in front of her.

"Let me help you with that. I think it's my turn to take care of you."

He gently removed the rest of her clothes, leaving her bare for him to see. Her eyes glanced down and found him already hard, his cock straining against his briefs. She bit her lip as she stepped forward. Reaching down, she tucked her hands beneath the edge of his underwear to push them down, freeing his hardened length. She licked her lips at the sight of the long length of him, and the deep colored mushroom tip.

He took her hand and guided her into the shower. The warm water beat down on her sensitive skin. She could barely take her eyes off him as he reached around her for the soap. He lathered his hands and started with her shoulders. She stood still, facing him, their eyes locked as he began to sensually wash her.

This was way better than when she did him, she thought to herself. She at least got to be awake for this sensual torture.

She released a moan as his large hands drifted down to her aching breasts. Her mounds ached to feel his tongue wrapped around her nipples, but she knew she would have to be patient. His massive hands gripped her soft flesh and massaged as much as he washed. The color of his eyes deepened as he continued lower.

The water beat down on her back while steam filled the air, but Ilena was oblivious to anything else outside of Remus's hands on her.

Her pussy pulsed as he continued. He knelt down in front of her, and she trembled with every caress of his hands. His hands took their sweet time running the length of her short legs.

"Turn," he murmured.

She did as he instructed, bracing her hands on the wall. The water continued to flow down her back, but it didn't stop him as he made his way up her legs. She jumped at the slight nip of her butt cheek with his sharp fangs.

"Hey," she chirped, but then moaned as his slippery hands made their way to her ass to soothe where he had bitten her. He gently spread her cheeks, ensuring that every part of her was clean. Her pussy dripped with wetness as he cleaned between her ass cheeks.

She needed to feel him inside of her. She felt him shift to stand behind her, then his hands reached around to grip her breasts as he pulled her back against his chest.

Remus groaned as his cock brushed against her slippery ass. She shifted her hips, purposely brushing against him again. He buried his head in the crook of her neck as he massaged her breasts.

"Spread your legs."

She did as he asked. He shifted his hips and she felt the hardened length slip between her cheeks to rub against her slick entrance. Her body continued to shake with need as he teased her, moving his cock against her entrance. Her pussy clenched, waiting for the moment he would thrust into her.

"Remus," she moaned as one of his hands found its way to her folds. She reached up and gripped his hair with one of her hands, needing something to hold onto to keep her from falling.

His fingers dove in, finding her swollen flesh and began to work her clit.

"What do you want?" he asked, dragging his fangs against her neck.

"You know what I need," she gasped, her eyes rolling into the back of her head as she rode his fingers. She groaned, tucking this memory into the back of her mind. *He wanted to play teasing games? Well, she would pay him back.* Oh, she would definitely pay him back one day. Two could play this game.

"Tell me," he demanded, sinking his teeth into her neck.

A deep moan escaped her as he fed from her. She spread her legs wider, needing more. He shifted again, and this time, his cock thrust into her. Her pussy greedily took him in. Her walls clenched around him as he fed her every inch of him. The movement caused her to tip forward, but she caught herself, bracing her hands against the wall as he released her neck. His cock seated deep within her pulsed. If she didn't know any better, she would have sworn that he swelled even more as she clenched her muscles again, gripping him tighter in her sheath. He licked her neck to seal the wound closed as he thrust again, gripping her breasts tight in his hands.

"Tell me what you want," he repeated as he thrust harder.

She could barely formulate a conscious word, and yet he wanted her to answer an important question such as this.

"Everything," she ground out. "Give me everything."

CHAPTER SIX

~ Remus ~

The softness of her skin just about drove Remus crazy. Yes, they had just met, but everything about Ilena was perfect for him. Her height, the size of her breasts that filled his large hands just right, and the feel of her pussy walls clenching him with every stroke. Even her slight Spanish accent was just fucking perfect.

He sent a quick prayer to the Gods for sending him his mate. He didn't know who he tortured more with washing her, him or her. His cock practically begged to enter her. His hands shook as he took his time discovering every facet of her skin.

He couldn't get enough of her. Her muttered words switched over to Spanish, and for once in his life, he would give his left arm to be able to speak the language. A hot bolt of lightning shot up from the base of his scrotum as his release began to build. His hands slipped across her soapy skin as he tried to thrust even deeper.

She protested as he withdrew from her hot center. He quickly spun Ilena around and easily lifted her up by the back of her knees. She grunted as he pressed her back against the wall and lined his cock up with the slick folds of her pussy.

"Everything?" he asked, thrusting back home. He wanted to see her face this time as he took her. His cock slid easily into her slick core.

"Yes," she groaned, her walls clenching him tight with each thrust. He increased his pace, unable to look away from her dark eyes as she wrapped her arms around his neck. The sounds of her moans and gasps filled the air. He was quickly becoming addicted to the sounds of his mate in the throes of passion.

"It's yours," he promised. His muscles began to tremble and he refused to orgasm without her. He reached down with one hand and slid his finger into her slick folds, finding her swollen nub. He applied just enough pressure to tip her over. Ilena's head fell back against the wall as her muscles clenched. She cried out as she reached her peak, with him right behind her, shouting his.

"We really shouldn't stay in bed all day." Ilena's

voice was muffled as she nuzzled Remus's bare chest.

"Really?" Remus murmured, tilting her chin up with his finger. He lowered his mouth and covered hers, unable to keep his hands or mouth off of her. She moaned as the kiss deepened as her small hands found their way up to his neck and dove into his hair. Her sharp tug had him wanting to roll them until he could settle between her thighs.

A stirring between his legs let him know that he could easily go again, but she was right. They couldn't stay in bed all day. Ryan was kind enough to give them a day together. Over the past twenty-four hours, they had barely come up for air. In-between their lovemaking, they'd learned of each other, and how much they were alike.

But, he still had a job to do. They would have an eternity to be together and learn more of each other. He regretfully broke the kiss.

"You're right," he acknowledged, placing another sweet kiss on her lips before pulling back.

"I am?" she asked, with a dazed look in her eyes. Her swollen lips had him craving more, but he knew that they would have to leave their quarters soon.

He had to report to the king tonight for his assignment. Even though he was newly mated with Ilena, he still had a job to do, to secure the future of vampires everywhere. He couldn't think of a future with Ilena without thinking of his race.

"I have to report to work tonight," he

announced, getting out of bed. The cool air brushed against his naked skin as he walked to the windows. Their windows were coated with a special tint to protect vampires from the sun. He peeked through the blinds and discovered that the sun had went down and dusk was upon them.

"As do I," Ilena said. He could hear the rustle of the covers as she exited the bed. Her soft footsteps approached him, then her warm arms wrapped around him, her ample breasts crushed against his back. "I'll miss you while you're gone."

His heart stuttered with the admission. He turned to find her dark eyes beaming up at him with a twinkle in her eyes. It felt damn good to know that now, when he came home weary from battle, or a hard day of service for his people, he would have a loving mate to come home to. His eyes roamed her honey skin—every curve, especially the plump brown mounds now crushed against his chest.

"You will be forever on my mind," he assured, gathering her naked form closer to him. The feel of her legs wrapped around his waist, and the feel of her moist center clenching around his cock would play in his mind forever. He lifted her in his arms and carried her back toward the bed. He just needed one more taste.

One for the road.

CHAPTER SEVEN

~ Ilena ~

"Ilena, dear," Bernia called out. Ilena quickly finished putting the new supplies that the infirmary had received on the shelves. She threw the empty box in the corner as she walked out of the supply closet.

"Yes, Bernia?" she responded as she walked toward the main bay. This night had been a slow one, and her thoughts had been consumed by Remus. She'd had a silly grin on her face the whole night so far. Bernia and the other nurses had been teasing her since she returned to work.

There it was again.

Her smile just would not leave her face. She was truly happy, and if she didn't know any better, she would say that she was in love.

Her feet paused at the realization. Her heart sped up with just the thought of him, and the memory of him thrusting deep inside of her had her core clenching.

Yes, she was a vampire in love.

"Ilena," Bernia's voice called out again.

"I'm coming," Ilena responded. Quickly turning the corner, she came to an abrupt halt.

Queen Summer was standing in the middle of the main bay of the infirmary with Bernia and two other nurses, Merle and Kismet, who she had become fast friends with in her short time at the royal mansion.

"Your Grace." Her voice ended on a squeak as she bowed her head to the queen out of respect.

"Ilena, how are you?" The queen asked as she made her way to Ilena.

"I'm doing well, Your Grace," she replied, feeling her smile spreading across her face. She groaned internally. Of course, the day she meets the queen, she would be a smiling fool.

"I told ya, Your Grace." Bernia laughed, along with Merle and Kismet. Ilena could feel her cheeks warm at the running joke. She could care less what they thought, though. Every joke was worth it when she thought of Remus and his hands on her, bringing so many smiles to her face today.

"Oh, leave the girl alone, Bernia." Queen Summer laughed, grabbing Ilena's hand.

Ilena's eyes widened and her heart rate increased. She couldn't believe how beautiful the queen was in person, or that she was holding her hand.

"It's okay," Ilena said.

"Don't mind them. I recognize that look on your face," Summer said with a small squeeze of her hand. "I was once in your position not too long ago, when Ryan and I found each other. So go ahead, be happy!"

"Yes, Your Grace," Ilena said, her face almost hurting from smiling.

"Now, the reason that I'm here..." Summer winked at Ilena before releasing her hand. She motioned for Ilena to follow her as she walked over to the center of the room. Ilena quickly made her way to them, confused as to what they could need her for. She doubted the queen would come to the infirmary to tell the other nursing staff to lay off the teasing.

"The king is arranging for the king's guards to invade the last laboratory. This one, we discovered, still has captive vampires. From what Zeke reported when he returned this morning is that some are in bad shape. We want a medical team to go with the guards," the queen informed.

"The queen has asked me to choose my best nurse to go with the medical team, and Ilena, I know that you are new to us, but I have chosen you," Bernia supplied. "You have jumped back into the world of nursing as if you'd never left."

"I'd be honored to help in any way that I can." Ilena's smile faltered.

All laughter faded from the room at the seriousness of the situation that Ilena and the medical team would embark on. Between the walls of the infirmary, they could forget for just a while about what was going on in the real world. Yes, it was a beautiful thing for two vampires to find each other, but there were so many that had suffered at the hands of the hunters.

Ilena looked around the room and nodded her head. She would do whatever she could to help her people. She had been a vampire on the run, so she knew what it was like to feel scared and hopeless. It was time for her to serve her people.

"This building is located in the heart of downtown. It's been beneath our noses and we wouldn't have ever known had the humans not given us the addresses." The king spoke to the group that would be rescuing the imprisoned vampires.

Ilena paid close attention to the king's words. She had already been briefed by Dr. Cain on what would be expected from the medical team. Her and a few others had been chosen to stay behind and man the portable medical station. She glanced up, taking in the moon high in the sky. She jumped slightly at the feeling of a familiar figure pressing close against her.

Remus.

"Are you going to be okay?" he asked as she turned to him.

"Yes, I should be." Worry filled her chest at the sight of him, decked out in his tactical gear. She gulped as the realization of his job set in. Before, when she caught a glimpse of him lying on the cot in the infirmary, it hadn't hit home. He was just a stranger who had been injured. But tonight, he was no longer a stranger; he was her mate. Her future. The love of her life.

Tonight, it was clear as a starless night sky. He could die saving the trapped vampires. A voice called out that it was time, and panic began to set in.

"It's time for me to go. Stay close to the med station and you should be safe," he said. He placed a kiss on her forehead and stepped back.

"Wait!" She grasped the tactical vest that protected his chest, the same item that had saved his life before, protecting him in order for them to find each other. Her hand moved to where his heart beat. She closed her eyes, feeling the warm trail of tears slide down her face. "Promise that you'll come back to me."

He stepped closer to her and gently grabbed her face in both of his large hands. He wiped the tears from her face as he gazed down at her.

"Don't worry, love," he murmured. "Nothing will keep me from returning to you."

CHAPTER EIGHT

~ Remus ~

"This time, let's try not to set off any traps," Zeke murmured as they crept through the building. The building that housed the imprisoned vampires was located in an abandoned warehouse on the outskirts of downtown. Remus had to force thoughts of Ilena's tear-filled eyes out of his mind so that he could concentrate on the task at hand.

He was left speechless with the emotions displayed on her face. It solidified that no matter what, he would return to her.

"Well, that means you need to watch where you put your big feet," he replied as they silently made their way into the building. A snort in front of him signaled that Zeke had heard him. But now that they were inside, they would go silent. The only communication would be from the communicators hidden in each of their ears to keep them connected to the others.

Zeke and Norrix had led a surveillance team the night before to learn about the building and its design. It came as a shock that the building still held hostages. Ever since Ryan had received the addresses to all the last testing facilities, they had hoped they would all be emptied out, but unfortunately, Zeke and Norrix discovered evidence that this one still had occupants. They had to act quickly and try to save the trapped vampires before they died of starvation. Since the human scientists abandoned most of the experimental laboratories, the vampires were left with no way out of their prison cells.

Against Ryan's protests, they all agreed that after the last mishap, he could not participate in the extraction of hostages. They could not risk their king being killed; he was the last royal member of his family. Norrix led a few other guards into the building through another entrance.

They moved effortlessly through the main lobby, toward the staircase, with their weapons raised. A sense of déjà vu set in as they paused beside the door. Zeke moved to the other side of the doorframe.

"We're in," Norrix's voice quietly said through the communicator.

Zeke's eyes met Remus's and they both nodded their heads at each other, signaling they were ready before he turned the handle. A soft click filled the air, and Zeke paused before pushing the door open.

Remus breathed deeply as he followed his friend into the darkened stairway. The hairs on the back of Remus's neck rose and stood at attention, and he paused on the stairwell. Zeke paused too, as if sensing Remus was no longer behind him.

"Something's wrong," Remus murmured as he went down a few more steps to catch up with Zeke.

"Your gut telling you something?" Zeke asked. Remus nodded, shifting his weapon in order to push on his communicator to speak.

"Ryan, come in," Remus said quietly into the communicator.

"Yeah, I'm here. What have you found?" Their king's voice cut in over the slight static.

"Something's off. Everything cool out there?" Remus asked, as flashes of Ilena's face came to mind.

Crackling noises was the only response.

"Ryan," he called out again, trying to keep his voice down.

Nothing but silence greeted them this time.

"Norrix, come in." Remus switched lines, attempting to get ahold of his commander. His heart sped up as his imagination began to run wild with all the things that could be going wrong on the outside.

Nothing but more static greeted them.

"Shit," Zeke cursed under his breath.

Communications were down. Something was

very wrong.

"Keep going. Norrix and the others are in the building," Remus murmured. There were other guards protecting the king and everyone who was outside, waiting for them to extract the trapped vampires.

Zeke nodded and continued the trip down the dark staircase. Remus knew his longtime friend didn't like the fact that they had no communication with the others, but they still had a job to do. It was up to them to save their people.

They exited the stairwell and found themselves in an open area that was once used as offices, with empty cubicles spread out around the room. Zeke pointed to a glass door in the back that was labeled "Lab." They made their way toward it, assessing the room for hidden dangers.

Zeke nodded to the electronic swipe pad. Remus flipped his silencer on, stepped back and took aim. One shot later and the security panel was destroyed. The door clicked, allowing Zeke to push it open. They slowly walked through the door, finding themselves entering a breezeway into the official lab. They walked past the white lab coats that hung on hooks, then opened the door that led into the main laboratory.

The sterile room was open with large cots that Remus could tell were for vampires. Leather straps lied across the beds that were used to secure the vampires. Medical equipment, monitors, and unfamiliar devices were strewn around the room.

His eyes landed on a contraption that stood tall in the middle of the room. He walked toward it and examined it, discovering headrests that were carved out of the metal where a person's head would rest. He looked up and found a plastic covering that would drop over the vampire's head. Again, leather straps hung from this machine as well, along with IV tubing.

His stomach grew queasy with the thoughts of what was done to the vampires in this room. He looked around the room, taking in the glass encased prison cells that lined the walls.

"What in the hell?" Zeke murmured, coming to stand next to Remus.

The sound of the door opening grabbed their attention, causing them to aim their weapons toward the door, just as Norrix walked through with his weapon trained on them.

"What the fuck?" he exclaimed, coming to an abrupt halt. The other guards, Vox and Mouri, dropped their weapons as they entered the room.

"Why aren't the communicators working?" Zeke asked as Norrix walked over to them.

"Haven't a fucking clue," Norrix hissed, his eyes locked on the torture machine. "They've never malfunctioned before."

That didn't sit well with Remus. That feeling in his gut was back. He needed to go back up top. He didn't know how he knew, but in the back of his mind, a warning sound was blaring in his head. Something was definitely wrong.

"Are we too late?" Vox asked.

They all looked around the room at the cells. There was no movement inside of them, so Remus sent up a prayer that they weren't too late.

"Ryan, come in." Norrix spoke into his communicator in an attempt to reach the king.

The plan had been designed that once the guards had deemed the building safe, Dr. Cain and a few of his staff would come down and assess the vampires before they were transported.

Norrix cursed under his breath.

"Nothing?" Remus asked.

"No. Let's grab whoever is alive and get them out. Whatever is going on up top, we'll deal with once we're out. It's too dangerous to stay down here."

CHAPTER NINE

~ Remus ~

Remus burst through the door that led outside. They had exited the building through the way that Norrix and his men had entered. Zeke was behind him, carrying one of the survivors over his shoulder. The sounds that greeted them had the bottom of his stomach falling out. The sounds of gunfire filled the air as they made their way down a dark alley, off to the side of the building.

They took off in a dead run down the alley and around the corner. The med station was one block away.

Ilena.

He ran faster, pumping his arms hard as he ran toward the fight, leaving Zeke behind. He had to save his mate. He promised her that he would come back to her.

He didn't care about the dangers he was running into. It didn't matter. He had to ensure that she was safe. He made it to the location of the medical station and slowed down to a jog as he took in the sight in front of him.

Complete mayhem had ensued.

He beat down the panic that started to set in as he aimed his weapon and shot a human who walked out from behind the station. Remus didn't care why the human was there. No humans were supposed to be in the area, so that meant he was one of them.

The hunters.

Humans set on killing his people. This explained why they didn't have communication with the topside. The humans must have cut communication and attacked while they were rescuing the imprisoned vampires.

The man's body flew back, his gun falling from his hand. Remus stalked toward him and kicked the gun away. The human's eyes were glassed over, frozen in death. He glanced around the area, not seeing anyone else.

Where the hell was Ilena and the king?

"Ryan!" Remus called out, shouting for his king. It looked as if there was an explosion. A few of the vampires that were waiting to help were lying on the ground, deep burns covering their bodies. Moans and cries filled the area as Remus walked around, looking for anyone who could be a threat.

"Remus!" Ryan's voice broke through Remus's thoughts. He swung around and found Ryan motioning to him from behind the back area of the station. He moved through, keeping his gun up high in case more of the hunters showed themselves. When he reached where Ryan knelt, he fell to his knees.

Ilena, burned and barely conscious, sat propped up against a stack of the trunks that held the medical supplies.

"Ilena," he gasped, forgetting all that was around them. "What happened?" he demanded to know as he gathered her to his chest.

"Remus," she gasped, reaching up to clutch his vest. Her body trembled as she held onto him.

"The fucking hunters came and threw grenades into the station and attacked. But these grenades were something we've never seen before. It was like the explosion emitted sunlight." Ryan's voice ended on a growl as he sat on the ground.

"You made it back," Ilena said in awe.

"Don't speak," he murmured, brushing her hair away from her face. He tried to rein in his anger, not wanting to scare her. He reached up and wiped away a trail of blood from her temple. "It's going to be all right."

"I knew you would make it back to me," she whispered, shifting her head back so her eyes could meet his. Her eyes were wide and glossy. Shock was settling in. He would need to get her medical attention soon. "I prayed that you would make it out of the building."

"I'm here," he assured her, shifting her body in his arms to free one of his arms. She would need blood to help the healing process. He placed his wrist against her lips, encouraging her to feed. Her small fangs pierced his flesh, allowing her to drink. His blood would give her the strength she would need to begin the healing process. Whatever new weapon these humans had burned her and the others, as if they were thrust into sunlight.

With the help of blood, she would heal, and there would be no scars, thanks to their vampire DNA. His heart swelled as he held her close. He could hear shouts from his teammates making their way to the med station. Ryan stood and walked off, patting Remus on the shoulder to meet the other royal guards. They would ensure that the rest of the group was safe.

He glanced back down and found her eyes locked on his. "I told you, nothing would keep me from coming back to you."

EPILOGUE

~ Ilena ~

A few weeks had passed since the attack on the med station. Ilena sighed, thinking back to that night. She had been scared when the humans attacked. If it hadn't been for the king, she didn't know if she would be here now. She was one of the lucky ones. Her worst injuries were from the grenades, causing second and third degree burns. It took a few days of rest and blood to heal, but her body had returned to its normal state.

Remus had been glued to her hip, afraid to leave her alone as she healed and recovered. He blamed himself. She'd tried to convince him that he wouldn't have known that something was wrong, but he swore that his gut told him something was, and that he should have come back to investigate it.

After they had transported all the injured to the local supernatural hospital that had recently opened, the building was burned down. Remus refused to tell her what they had found down there. She shuddered as she made her way to the main bay, trying to block out the images her imagination was conjuring up. She didn't even want to guess what was down in that laboratory.

It took a lot of convincing to prove that she was ready to return to work; she was dying to get back. "Surprise!" voices yelled out, causing Ilena to jump as she entered the main area of the infirmary. Streamers and balloons lined the ceiling, with a sign that read *Welcome Back*. Tears welled up in her eyes as she took in all her co-workers. Smiles lined their faces as the tears ran down her face.

"Welcome back, dear." Bernia laughed as she walked over to hug her. Ilena returned the hug, squeezing the head nurse tight. She felt love from everyone in the room as they all rushed over to her with smiles and hugs, just to welcome her back.

Ilena smiled through her tears as she thought about everything that she'd been through over the past ten years, and up until this moment. It was worth it, and it was meant to be. Destiny had a plan for her, and led her to exactly where she needed to be.

~ The End ~

NICIA'S DESTINY

AN EROTIC VAMPIRE SERIES, VOL. 4

CHAPTER ONE

~ Zeke ~

"Our own people feel that we're not doing enough," Ryan snapped as he paced the room. Zeke Galanis silently watched as his king grew agitated. Ryan Valerian was the last surviving member of the royal family, the rightful king of all vampires, and he was pissed. The boardroom of the king's mansion was filled with only the top royal guards: Norrix, the commander of the guards, Remus, and Zeke. They were the closest to the king, and this meeting was for only the highest guards.

"Not everyone is turning on you," Norrix said from his spot at the table. Norrix and Ryan were longtime friends. If there was anyone, aside from the queen, that could calm him down, it was

Norrix. "You know there have always been groups that will be against the crown."

"Only this group is gaining supporters. She has a following," Ryan spat, turning to the group. "We need a meeting with her."

Zeke turned his attention back to the screen on the wall that displayed a photo of the object of their conversation.

Nicia Springson was a strong female vampire who fought for their race. The video that was captured showed her in the middle of a fight, and Zeke had to resist the urge to adjust himself. He shook his head and laughed to himself as he willed his cock to go down. He had to admit that she was very attractive, and watching a woman wield a dagger with the precision of an assassin, downright turned him on. Maybe he just needed to get laid. It had been a few days, and he was sure that he could find someone to scratch his itch.

But his eyes were drawn back to the screen. She may have unconventional ways, but she had the hunters running, something they had been unable to do. Instead, the hunters had been getting uncomfortably close to their camp. A month ago, the hunters attacked while he and the other royal guards were trying to rescue vampires trapped in an abandoned laboratory. With their new weapon, sun grenades, many vampires had been injured, including Remus's mate, Ilena.

"Will she agree to meet with you?" Norrix asked, tapping his fingers on the table.

"I'm her king. She damn well better meet with me," Ryan growled as he sat down in his chair at the head of the table.

"Why not let someone else go first and speak with her?" Remus asked. Zeke's ears perked at the mention of someone traveling to meet with the vampiress, but Remus would probably volunteer to go speak with her. He had a way about him that drew people to him. Maybe he could make Nicia accept Ryan's invitation. "I know that you two go back a ways and know each other, but I think that right now, tempers are flying with all the attacks of the hunters. Vampires shouldn't be at odds with each other."

"He's right," Zeke said, speaking up for the first time. Being in the middle of war with the hunters, this was not the time to fight against each other. If they were to win the war, all vampires must be on the same side. Again, he found his eyes on the frozen image of Nicia. Something stirred in his chest as his eyes rested on the raven-haired beauty.

"So, you'll go and inform her that her king is requesting an audience with her?" Ryan asked, his eyes locked on Zeke.

Zeke's eyes met his king's. He knew right now that he would not be able to deny him. Ryan's fuse was two seconds from detonating and Zeke, fierce warrior that he was, knew not to cross him.

"Yes, Your Grace." He groaned internally. He didn't know why he was having this draw to Nicia, so he pushed it down. He didn't like it, whatever it

193

was. He looked around the room and knew that he was the only unmated male at the table. Ryan, Norrix, and Remus, all had found their destined mates. It wasn't that Zeke was angry that his fellow vampires had found their other halves; it was that he knew he wasn't made to have another half.

Finding a mate was not in the cards for him. Not that he was searching or anything. Zeke Galanis would be an unmated vampire for the rest of his days on this Earth.

~ Nicia ~

She would show this dummy no mercy. *You fought how you practiced.* This was something that was drilled into her head from the moment she began her training. Sweat poured off her face as she alternated solid punches. Her biceps tensed as she landed yet another hard blow to the chest of the dummy. She paused, sensing someone had entered the small workout room. She turned to find her longtime friend and guard, Despina, had entered the room.

Nicia Springson was the daughter of the late Pavlos and Jacinta Springson. Both her parents were killed during the initial attacks of the hunters. Vampires had been so used to being at the top of the food chain, that when the attacks happened, they were not prepared. The hunters were a human group determined to wipe out vampires from the face of the Earth.

Ever since the attacks, she had fought against the humans, trying to save her people. She had refused to run and hide. During the wave of the first attacks, she had made it home to her parents' house, where she'd made a gruesome discovery, finding her parents dead in their home. Their bodies had been tortured with sunlight until they could take no more. It was Nicia who buried her parents in the family cemetery. It was she who had made sure that their final resting place was with family. Through all the years of destruction and chaos, Nicia had defended her family's estate, refusing to cower to the humans.

Nicia would have her revenge. Every human hunter she killed brought her only a pinch of satisfaction. She would not be satisfied until every single one of the hunters were dead.

"Despina," she greeted as she paused her brutal workout. She turned to find her friend patiently leaning against the doorjamb.

"You have a visitor," Despina announced, folding her arms across her chest. Nicia didn't like the smirk that had taken up residence on Despina's face. She looked down at herself and knew that a sports bra and leggings weren't the proper attire to greet a guest in.

"Who?" she asked as she reached for her towel on the floor. She scooped it up and began wiping her face and neck.

"You'll just have to see." Despina chuckled as she turned away and disappeared through the door.

"You know I don't like surprises," Nicia snapped, a little irritated with her friend as she threw the towel over her shoulder. She turned and dragged the rubber man back into the corner where it belonged.

She turned and paused, finding Despina had returned quickly, but this time, she had a guest with her. His face looked slightly familiar to her, but she couldn't place where she had seen him before. Her breath got stuck in her throat as her eyes took him in. This was definitely a warrior, someone who had seen battle before. Looking at his clothes, she saw the royal emblem on the shoulder of his dark jacket.

A royal guard.

She scowled at the realization that this was one of the king's men. Just thinking of the king made Nicia's fists clench. He was *not* her king. A true king would never have abandoned his people. All those years that Ryan had been missing, everyone had assumed he was dead, including herself. She had mourned for her dear, childhood friend. Once he reappeared, she had lost all respect for him. Here she was, fighting for their people, while he hid away like a coward.

"Nicia, this is Zeke Galanis, one of the top royal guards to King Ryan Valerian," Despina announced, waving a hand at the oversized vampire. "This is Nicia Springson."

"What do you want?" Nicia snapped. She and the king had practically grown up together. His parents had been close friends with hers. The Springson's had always had a seat on the council, and with the deaths of her parents, the seat was rightfully hers. But during the last ten years, the council had been nonexistent with so many vampires being hunted down. From what she had heard, only a few remained.

"I'll leave you two alone." Despina sighed as she walked out of the room, shaking her head.

"Why are you here?" Nicia asked. The heat of his gaze aroused her and sent a chill down her spine. "Well, are you going to answer me?"

She put her hands on her hips and tapped her foot. She didn't have all day. She had a million things to do, and having a staring match with a sexy vampire was not one of them.

"We are not the enemy."

CHAPTER TWO

~ Nicia ~

Her feet slowly carried her toward the vampire.
The rugged shadow on his jawline made her
fingers itch. Something drew her to him. His hazel
eyes deepened as she stopped in front of him. She
tilted her head back so that she could look up into
his eyes.

Shit.

In her mind, she knew she shouldn't give in to
her traitorous body, but how could she not? He
was well over six feet tall, body of a warrior, and
her pussy clenched as he gazed down at her.

"I never accused you of being the enemy, unless
Ryan has decided to side with the humans." She
cocked an eyebrow at him. She tried to keep her
breathing to a normal rate, but it was proving to be

hard as her body responded to his. She watched, fascinated, as his nostrils flared.

Yeah, he was affected by her too.

"Ryan would never do that," he snapped.

"I heard that he'd had a meeting with the human government. A year after the epic return of the vampire king, and vampires are still second-class citizens." She turned to move away from him, but his hand shot out and grabbed her arm, holding her in place. She looked at him with an eyebrow cocked.

"Let me go," she warned, her fist clenching. Little did he know she was moving away from him for fear of her body thrusting itself at him. Today, she was learning how quick her body could turn on her.

"Look, you know Ryan. From what I know, you two were raised together and used to be friends—"

"Key word, *used to be*," she snapped, snatching her arm away and turning back to him. Her anger peaked. He knew nothing of her and her childhood. Who was he to bring up the relationship between Ryan and her?

"He sent me to request your presence at the king's mansion."

"So he sent you, an errand boy." She poked his chest with her finger. It was like stabbing a steel wall. Her core pulsed with the thought of what was beneath his clothing. He gripped her wrist in his larger hand as his eyes burned into hers.

"I'm no errand boy," he growled, his fangs

peeking from beneath his lips.

"Here you are." She poked again, knowing that she had his number. She licked her lips and watched as his eyes traced the movement of her tongue. She just couldn't help taunting him. The sexual tension in the air was so thick, it could have been sliced with a knife. "An errand boy."

His hand shot out and grabbed her by her neck. He applied just a slight pressure to assert his dominance. Her pussy clenched again as he leaned forward to where his lips brushed hers. She wasn't worried about his hand on her throat. She knew she could get out of this easily. His show of dominance had the moisture practically leaking from her pussy.

"You don't know when to quit, do you?" he growled, his eyes locked on hers.

Her heart raced as images of him thrusting hard inside of her came to mind. She knew he wanted her by the glint that appeared in his eyes the moment she walked over to him. He squeezed ever so slightly on her neck, and she knew that having sex with him would be a rough tumble. Thank the heavens above she was built tough and could handle him.

Her lips curved up into a sensual smile as she whispered the following words. "Boy."

He crushed his lips to hers in a bruising kiss. His tongue pushed its way into her mouth as a fierce army would invade an enemies' territory. Rough sex always helped her release built-up tension, and from the looks of Zeke, he would be the perfect partner to help her out.

Her hands reached up and pushed his jacket from his shoulders. He shrugged the jacket off, leaving him in his button-down shirt. The sounds of material ripping filled the air as he pulled on her sports bra, tearing the shoulder straps.

She broke the kiss and gasped as her breasts became free of their restraint. The cool air caused her nipples to harden into sensitive little buds. He trailed hot kisses along her jawline, toward the crook of her neck. Her gums began to burn as her fangs broke through and descended.

She threaded her fingers into his hair as she backed up. He followed her, a predator after it's prey. Cool brick met her back as he backed her up against the wall. The need to bite him was strong, but she pushed it to the back of her mind. She felt him pull away from her, causing her to open her eyes, and found him staring down at her.

~ Zeke ~

Zeke tried to control his breathing, but his heart was racing too fast. The warning bells were screaming in the back of his mind. This was not the woman to screw around with, but the taste of her salty skin had him ready to take her against the wall of her sparring gym. His hands slid up to her bare breasts, her dark nipples begging for his touch. He glanced down at her, unsure for the first time in his life if he should bed a female. His hands covered her plump globes, finding that they filled his large hands perfectly. He teased her unmercifully by stroking her beaded nipples, then pinching them tight, causing her head to fall back against the wall with her eyes closed in ecstasy.

She was the old friend of the king. She may be pissed at Ryan, but he was still supposed to bring her to him. Ryan would have his balls if he found out that he was currently groping his childhood friend. Had this been any other woman, he would have her pinned up against the wall before she could blink.

"Why did you stop?" she asked. Her eyes were filled with lust, and her hands were making light work of his pants. He had to fight the pull, but he couldn't. He cursed under his breath for not finding a female before his trip to let loose his pent-up aggression. He thought that this mission would be quick and painless.

"We shouldn't. The king—"

"What happens between us is no one's business, especially Ryan's," she murmured, her hand sliding into his pants. Her hands pushed his pants down, just enough for her to go exploring. His breath caught in his throat as her hand encircled his cock. Sweat trailed down his temples as she slid her hand down the length of him. She released a groan at the size of him. He could feel his cock jump at the feel of her small hand encircling him. "You're a big boy. I'm sure you can make your own decisions, and from the feel of you right now in my hand, you want to fuck me."

He released a deep groan as she pulled his cock from his pants. "Nicia—"

"Admit it," she teased as she slid to her knees. Nicia was a highborn vampire, the heir to her father's council seat. A council that was once as powerful as the king, yet too had perished after the attacks from the hunters. Over the past decade, Nicia was one of the only council heirs that was known to have survived. She was one of the most powerful female vampires in the world, and here she was, in front of him on her knees with his cock in her hand. He swallowed hard as he felt his cock swell even more. The sight of this highborn on her knees was a complete turn on for him. "You want me," she breathed.

His eyes followed her body and he watched, frozen in place, as her lips closed around the head of his cock.

"Fuck, yeah."

Any thought of what his king would think flew out the window. Ryan didn't need to know what went on between him and Nicia. She was a willing female who was begging him to fuck her, and he would. He threaded his fingers in her hair as he guiding his cock further into her mouth. He hissed as she took him deep into her throat.

He'd planned to show her how he liked for his

cock to be sucked, but as she pulled back and began to stroke him with her tongue, he could tell that she wouldn't need his guidance. His body trembled as she twirled her tongue along the mushroom tip. He spread his legs wider to better his footing as she worked him well enough to send chills down his spine.

"Open your mouth wider," he demanded around a deep groan, as he increased his tempo of fucking her mouth. Her mouth was exquisite. It took everything that he gave without complaint.

This had to be the best mission he'd ever been sent on. He couldn't for the life of him think of any better. Her free hand slid its way up his legs and gently cupped his ball sack, drawing a gasp from him. She gently rolled them in her hands, as if testing the weight before her gentle grasp applied a slight pressure.

Her hands and mouth worked in tandem as she brought him to the brink of euphoria. The hand that was wrapped around the base of his cock slid effortlessly along his shaft from the saliva that coated it. He cursed as he felt that familiar tingling sensation at the base of his balls. He looked around the room, trying to find something to distract him and keep him from releasing so soon, but he failed.

"Hold that thought," he murmured. He refused to release his seed so quick into her hot little mouth. He wanted to feel her pussy grip him. If they only got this one chance to fuck, he wanted to say that he'd been balls deep in a highborn.

Zeke reached down and grabbed her by her arms and pulled her to a standing position. He crushed his mouth to hers in bruising kiss. His hands reached down and slid her pants from her body, practically ripping them off in the process. She weighed next to nothing, and made it easy for him to lift her up and slam her against the wall. His cock didn't need any help finding her wet core.

"Yes," she hissed, throwing her head back with her eyes closed. His gums burned as his fangs broke through again. He ached to sink his fangs deep into her plump jugular artery that pulsed just beneath her skin, but he was able to restrain himself.

He thrust home, gripping her thighs tight in his hands. He released a shout as a feeling he'd never experienced before burst forth in his chest. He pulled back and thrust again, needing to be closer to her. The overwhelming feeling of needing to consume her overcame him. He'd never experienced this type of emotion in the throes of sex before.

"Harder. You know you can fuck me harder than that," she gasped, threading her fingers into his hair as he granted her wish.

This was one of the things that he loved about vampires. Vampires were fast healers. When coupling, if it got a little rough, he never had to worry about the vampire females. They would heal extremely fast, and there would be no bruises left on his lovers after a night of overzealous passion.

206

Gripping her hair tight, he pulled her head back so that he could taste her salty skin again. He licked along her pulsing artery, tempted to take a taste, but he reined back his desire for blood. He shifted his hips and thrust harder, crushing her plump mounds to his chest.

"Goddess above," she chanted over and over. Her pussy gripped his cock tight, as if it didn't want to let him go. He couldn't understand why he was so pleased that he was the one to give her pleasure. Not that he was a selfish lover.

This time, it was different.

"Shit," he muttered against her skin as her pussy contracted around his length. Her hips met his stroke for stroke in a sensual rhythm.

He wasn't going to last much longer. He grew closer to his release as he felt his sack tighten. He didn't want to release without her, though. Zeke would be a gentleman and ensure that the councilwoman would find her release too. He dragged his fangs along her skin and felt a shudder pass through her.

She was right there on the edge.

Her blood was calling to him, and he could no longer fight the temptation to taste her. He sank his fangs into her jugular, causing her to scream as her orgasm slammed into her. Her body drew tight as she fell into her release. Her legs clamped tight around him as he continued to draw from her vein.

The taste of her coppery substance filled his mouth and released a rush of power that surged within him. He threw his head back and roared his release as he filled her with his seed.

CHAPTER THREE

~ Nicia ~

Nicia awoke to the feel of a talented tongue on her clit. Confusion clouded her mind at first, but then the memories of the sparring room returned and she remembered who she'd invited into her bed that evening.

Zeke.

After their tryst in the workout room, she had led him to her private suite that was located close by. Their lovemaking had continued in the shower, then ended in her bed.

"Yes," she hissed as he gently bit down on her sensitive nub. She spread her legs wider to ensure he had perfect access to her slippery core. He cupped his hands beneath her ass cheeks and lifted her up higher to him as he feasted on her sweetness.

His stamina was one that seemed to easily match hers. Ryan certainly knew which of his guards to send. Zeke's massive cock and talented tongue was enough to keep her busy for hours. She would definitely go and meet with her old friend, if only to thank him for sending Zeke to her. It had been a long while since she'd had a partner that pleased her so.

"Your pussy is so sweet," Zeke murmured against her plump lower lips, before spreading her lips and dipping his tongue deep into her pussy. She gasped as she felt his finger invade her core. He pulled his fingers out and spread her wetness around her pussy, then trailed his fingers to her anus. She glanced down and caught him licking his fingers as his dark eyes bored into hers from below. "This fucking cunt calls to me. I can eat it all day."

"You can eat it as long as you want, as long as you make me come again." She groaned as she felt pressure from his finger being introduced into her ass.

"Whatever the lady requests," he announced, his eyes roaming her body, pausing at her plump mounds before settling back on her exposed pussy.

He lowered his head and she felt the tip of his tongue on her sensitive nub as he pushed his finger deeper into her ass. She gasped at the invasion, but loved the feel of the pressure from behind as he paid close attention to her pussy's need. The combination of both sensations caused her hips to lift on their own, trying to offer all of her to him.

Zeke was a skilled lover, and presently, she would be willing to let him do just about anything to her. Her neck ached slightly, reminding her of him feeding from her earlier. Her fangs broke with the thought of returning the favor. She ached to sink her fangs into him. The call of his blood was strong.

She didn't know why, but she needed to consume his blood, yet currently, her body had a mind of its own and it was focused on the pleasure of Zeke's tongue. Her pussy pulsed as he increased the pressure on her clit. He sucked her nub hard, causing her to release a deep moan as he thrust his finger back and forth into her tight channel.

"Shit," she bit out around her fangs as her orgasm hit her again. Her legs clamped around him as she shook from the aftermath. Her breaths were coming fast as she watched him climb over her.

Her eyes locked with Zeke's before he leaned down and covered her mouth with his. She could taste herself on him and loved it. She reached up and threaded her fingers in his hair as he angled his mouth to deepen the kiss. He settled in-between her legs with his thick cock between them. The tip brushed against her soaked core, and she ached to have him fill her. She loved how he ensured that her pussy would be ready for his thick cock.

She shifted her hips and rubbed her slick pussy lips against it, trying to guide him where she needed him the most.

"Are you going to come with me to meet with the king?" he asked, pulling back slightly. Her breaths came fast and hard as she achingly waited to be filled by him. She cursed at his show of dominance over her again.

She loved it.

Little did he know, he had her wrapped around his little finger, but she'd be damned if she let him know that.

"Yes," she hissed around her fangs. His eyes connected with hers as he slammed his cock home. Yes, she would go with him to meet with Ryan, but only after she completely got her fill of Zeke.

~ Zeke ~

"Please, follow me," Zeke said, leading Nicia through the royal mansion. Nicia's two male guards, Stelios and Risto, trailed behind her as they walked down the main hall.

"You were one of the guards that stayed with Norrix and fought while our beloved king was hidden away?" she asked.

He stopped abruptly and turned to face her. She was a fierce vampiress in an all leather outfit and spiked stiletto heels. Even a night of passion with her wouldn't be enough to break his loyalty to the king.

"Quit it. You will respect my king in his home,"

he murmured, leaning in close to her. Her clear blue eyes narrowed on him before she nodded without a word. He eyed her large guards and dared them to say anything. She brushed past him, her heels clicking down the hallway.

"I used to run the halls of this house as a child. I probably know it better than you do. I don't need you to guide me. Is Ryan using his father's old office as his now?"

Stelios and Risto brushed past him, each bumping into his shoulder as they passed.

He sighed, running a hand across his face, knowing that he couldn't engage with them. She was here to bury the hatchet with Ryan. When they had finally come up for air and were able to keep their hands off each other, they were able to finally talk about why he was sent to her. Vampires needed to be united. Kicking both of her guards' asses would not solve their problem.

"Yes," he answered, pushing down his anger.

He would have to teach her manners. He caught sight of her ass in the leather pants as she turned the corner and knew that he would take great pleasure in it. He jogged and caught up to them. His hand reached for the office door first, beating Nicia's. She smirked as he leaned back against the door and stared down at her, not letting them in.

"Behave," he warned. He glanced at her guards, since the message was for them too. One wrong move on their part and truce be damned. He would protect his king.

"As much as I would like to smack Ryan upside his head, I can restrain myself. This is between my old friend and I," she announced, standing taller.

Even with her heels, the top of her head came to his chin. Her thick midnight hair hung down her back in waves. His fingers ached to grip it again, but now was not the time to be having carnal thoughts. He blinked a few times, trying to clear the images of her naked body from his mind.

"Do you have weapons on you?" he asked, not budging from his place in front of the door. The knob turned in his hand as the door opened.

Zeke turned to find Ryan standing behind him. He nodded his head in respect to his king as he moved his body from blocking the entrance to the office. Ryan returned the nod before his eyes turned to Nicia.

"She is not the enemy," Ryan announced as he stood in the doorway. "Nicia," he greeted her.

"It's been a long time, Ryan," Nicia said, her feistiness coming through as she placed her hands on her hips. Fire burned in her eyes as she stared at Ryan. Zeke stiffened as he waited for a smart comment to come from her mouth. For this vampiress to be a warrior for her people, she sure had a mouth on her.

Had she been any other woman on any other day, he would have loved her feistiness. He loved a woman full of fire and passion. That would be the type of woman he could settle down with—he froze at that train of thought.

What the fuck?

He was Zeke Galanis. He was not the mating type of vampire. Ryan, Norrix, and Remus may have found their other halves, but mating was not what was in the cards for Zeke. He would prefer to spend each night with a different woman. He had always preferred different tastes and being able satisfy whatever his cock desired for the night. But as his eyes locked on Nicia, a piercing pain entered his chest. He let loose a cough to suppress the pain.

What in the hell was that?

"And I see you haven't changed a bit," Ryan said dryly.

"But you have." Nicia's eyebrow arched as she stood before the king.

"We have much to discuss." Ryan moved to the side and waved her into the office.

"That we do, *old friend*," she murmured as she walked past them all. Ryan nodded to him as he closed the door behind them.

Zeke turned and eyed both vampires. This meeting better not last long. He wasn't much of a babysitter.

CHAPTER FOUR

~ Nicia ~

"Please, have a seat," Ryan said, waving her over to the chair in front of his desk.

She breathed a sigh of relief once the door was closed and she was no longer near Zeke. Whenever she was around him, she couldn't control herself. It was like she had a schoolgirl crush on him and just had to get under his skin to try to get him to notice her. She had a hard time reading him. She was used to men fawning all over her, but he was reserved, and she could see that he calculated everything.

"I see this room has barely changed," she said. She had many memories of being in this room as a child, when her father would come to speak with the king, Ryan's father. She glanced at the floor length windows and remembered a time where her and Ryan would sit there as innocent children. They would stare up at the moon, making up stories about it.

"Remember the story of the warrior landing on the moon?" Ryan asked softly. She turned and found him staring at the same spot and smiled, remembering the story that he had made up to tell her on one of the countless nights her father had come to be at the side of the king.

"That was a long time ago," she replied, her heart softening. They stared at each other before he broke the silence.

"I'm not perfect—" he started.

She held up her hand, not wanting to be an emotional female. She was a strong vampire who had fought for her people for the past decade. She refused to turn to mush and cry, sitting around with her childhood friend.

"None of us are. Ryan, I thought you were dead. Our people thought you had died. I mourned for you, prayed for you to have peace in the afterlife. Imagine how it felt to find out that a childhood friend, someone I cared for like a brother, who I thought was dead just reappeared out of thin air. Did you think you could just swoop in, rescue the vampire nation and everything was to be okay?"

He looked away from her and leaned back in his chair before turning back to her. Her heart ached for their people. She had done the best she could by trying to fill her father's shoes as a councilwoman and defending vampires. She'd heard that Norrix and the other royal guards had stayed and protected the royal mansion. It was a symbol of hope for their people, and she knew that the return of the vampire king was good for their people.

Zeke was right. If vampires were to succeed and defeat the hunters, then they would have to work together.

"There's not a day that I don't regret my decision to stay hidden. At the time, I thought that it was the best thing to do. If I stayed away, vampires would have risen together to fight against the hunters, but that idea backfired." He ran his hand through his hair and stood from his chair, walking over to the window next to the desk. "You have a lot of the vampire nation behind you. Thank you for being here for our people when I was not. That is what makes a good councilwoman."

"It was my duty. Sitting on the council was a right that came to me way too fast. I just did what I knew I was supposed to do."

"But still, vampires are flocking to you," he said, looking at her.

Her hardened heart cracked at the sight of Ryan's vulnerability. She knew he wouldn't show this side to just anyone. At that moment, she would have sworn his father was standing in front of her. She blinked a few times before standing from her chair. She placed her hands on the desk and leaned onto it.

"If vampires are going to rise, we're going to

219

have to work together," she announced. Yes, she may have a strong following, but he was still their king. She would ensure that her supporters would remain true to the crown. Vampires could not be at odds with each other. As a council member, it was her duty to support the king, even if she wanted to bash him upside the head at least once.

He turned to her and a devilish smile appeared on his face. This was the Ryan she knew and had grown up with.

"What do you have in mind?"

"I just so happened to have discovered where the hunters have made their base."

Nicia had heard of the last attack by the hunters on Ryan and his men as they had attempted to rescue vampires from an abandoned laboratory. She'd been tracking the hunters for months, and they had finally slipped up.

The human government may have denied having ties to this massive group of humans who were attacking vampires, but Nicia had a few insiders. The politicians all lied, and Nicia knew not to believe the show that the human government put on when they graced the television with their press releases. Her contact was able to go undercover, deep into the human's government, and was able to find out who the leader of the hunters was.

"And your contact is trustworthy?" Ryan asked as they all sat around the conference table in the windowless meeting room. She glanced around the room, taking in all the king's royal guards and hers, Stelios and Risto. They had been loyal to her and her family for years, and fought alongside her against the humans. Her eyes ended on Zeke.

Memories of his lips blazing a trail from her breasts to her core had her shifting in her seat. She had to push the memories to the back of her mind. His eyes darkened, as if knowing where her thoughts were. She quickly turned from him to answer Ryan's question.

"Yes, she is. She's worked for the government agency for years, and no one knows that she's actually a mixed breed. Her father was a vampire and her mother a human. I would like to keep her identity hidden. I promised her that I wouldn't tell anyone who she was for her protection."

"How has she not been discovered?" Norrix asked with a raised eyebrow.

"Easy. She can consume food, unlike us, so the humans haven't suspected anything. For everything that she's done for us, I will not break her trust," Nicia said, walking over to stand in front of the map.

She could feel Zeke's eyes on her and it literally sent a chill down her back. She glanced over in his direction and felt her pussy clench as her eyes met his. She tore her eyes from his and tried to catch her breath as she studied the map. She had to get her mind to planning their attack on the hunters and not sliding down on Zeke's magnificent cock again.

Dammit! There her mind went again! *Get ahold of yourself,* she murmured to herself.

"And we wouldn't ask you to break that confidence." Ryan nodded and joined her next to the map.

Nicia had met Addison Peck about eight years ago. Addison had been distraught that her father had been killed and was looking to exact revenge on the ones that killed him. She was away on business when the attacks had occurred, and had kept her heritage a secret for fear that they would kill her too. Addison, being part vampire, knew the hierarchy of vampires. With the king thought to be dead, she searched for any surviving council members and found Nicia.

Addison had sworn to help Nicia fight the hunters as long as she promised to keep her identity a secret. They both had felt that as long as Addison worked for the senator as a secretary, she would be able to feed Nicia information that would turn out to be extremely helpful.

"Here," she said, placing her finger on the map. "You did a good job destroying most of the hunter's bases and their labs that made their weapons that were used against us. But you didn't destroy them all. Giving you the names and locations of the labs that housed vampires was a distraction. There's one more. This is the head of their operations. While the government may have cut ties with them, they're still going strong. The leader of the hunters is a man named Stanley Kohl."

"I can't believe that they've been this close," he murmured in awe as he stared at the map.

"We've been tracking them for months," Stelios said from his spot in the room. "After the attack last month, they've settled for now. We think they're planning their next attack. That attack was to try to take you out, Your Grace."

Curses filled the air with that information.

"Here's a picture of him." Risto passed a picture of the human hunter around the room so that everyone could commit his face to memory. She had confidence that now, each vampire would remember the face of the man who helped kill so many of their kind.

"You're rise back to power has them scrambling. They didn't expect it," she said to her friend. "We need to plan an attack and get to them first before they have a chance to carry out whatever plan they have."

"I like the way she thinks," Remus said, tapping his fingers on the table. "We need to come up with a plan, and fast."

"Risto, please tell the room of the plan you developed." She motioned to her guard.

Everyone turned their eyes to him as both her and Ryan took their seats at the table. Risto had fought for her father and had always led their vampires into battle. She would trust him with her life, and had on more than one occasion.

The next few hours were spent developing the attack plan. It was simple, but brilliant. The humans wouldn't know what to expect. This would be an attack to end this war between the human hunters and vampires.

Nicia could feel her body grow weak. The sun must be about to rise. Vampires were nocturnal, unable to withstand the rays of sunlight, so they tended to sleep during the day. Nicia covered her mouth as a yawn escaped. She hadn't gotten much sleep yesterday, thanks to Zeke.

"Let's get some rest. Tonight, we hunt," Ryan announced, bringing the meeting to an end. "Nicia, you and your men are welcome to stay here for the day and rest. There is plenty of room."

"Thank you. That will be fine. Maybe it will give me time to meet your mate." She nodded as she stood. The room cleared out, leaving them alone.

"Yes. Summer has been dying to meet you." He smiled as they walked toward the door. "Can I ask you a question?"

She turned to him and found his eyebrow raised. She knew what he would ask, and she wasn't sure she wanted to answer the question. They had just rekindled their friendship. She wasn't sure if she was ready for him to start trying to play the role of big brother like he did when they were younger.

"I won't guarantee that you get an answer," she answered with a smirk.

"You and Zeke?"

"To that question, you will not get an answer."

CHAPTER FIVE

~ Zeke ~

Zeke couldn't stay away from Nicia. His feet carried him to her room in the royal mansion. Lucilla, the queen's personal servant, had escorted Nicia to her private quarters. It was a suite that was reserved for council members when they stayed at the mansion.

Zeke quickly picked the lock and let himself in, then quietly shut the door behind him. He needed to know what it was about her that drew him to her. The muffled sounds of a shower running could be heard. He cursed with the thought of what she would look like under the spray of water. Memories of yesterday popped in his head of them together in the shower.

His jeans grew tight as he made his way through

the sitting room and to the bedroom. Zeke tried to push all carnal thoughts aside. They needed to talk. He paused at the door as the sounds of the water shut off.

He walked over and stood by the treated windows and stared outside. Every window in the mansion had special tint on them to keep the rays of the sun from harming vampires.

A noise behind him grabbed his attention. He turned to find Nicia, fresh from her shower, standing inside the door of the bathroom. She had an expression on her face that mimicked his exact feeling.

Confused.

"Why can't I get you out of my mind?" he asked. One night spent together in her bed should have been enough. Usually, Zeke would have been on the prowl for his next sexual conquest by now.

"I don't know," she answered softly. Her eyes were wide as she stared at him. She was a perfect sight. Her dark, wet hair lied in waves around her shoulders as she stood before him in nothing but a towel. She looked like an innocent female, and not the dangerous warrior he had watched in films a few days ago. "I can feel it too."

He stared at her and it hit him, as to what destiny was trying to tell him. He shook his head and backed up slowly.

"No," he whispered, not wanting to accept what he could see before him.

She couldn't be. There was no way that destiny

was going to play a dirty trick on him and give him a mate, and a highborn vampiress at that. Someone above his class. Nicia stood still, not moving as the realization sunk in.

"You have got to be kidding me," she muttered, closing her eyes briefly.

"What?" he demanded to know. Now his curiosity was peaked. Did she not think that he would be good enough? Not that he wanted to settle down and mate, but if he did, he would make a perfect mate.

"It's been staring me in the face this whole time. The reason that when we first met, all I could think about was getting you in my bed," she said, shaking her head.

"And what is that?" he asked, already knowing what she would say. He ran a trembling hand through his hair, not exactly sure why destiny would want him to have a mate.

"It's destiny. I think you're my mate."

"And that's a problem?" he asked. Zeke wasn't sure why he suddenly wanted to know why she thought it was a bad thing.

"Well, I can see that you don't want a mate. If I were to mate with someone, he would first want to be with me," she said, tucking her towel tight around her as she walked into the room. She sat down in the plush chair next to the bed. "He would want to be by my side for all eternity. A life partner. Someone to cherish me, love me, and know how to pleasure me."

The thought of someone else touching her soft skin, tasting her sweet pussy, making her moan had him seeing red. He couldn't stand the thought of someone else touching what was his.

She belonged to him.

A growl vibrated from his chest as he stalked toward her. Her eyes widened as he reached her and pulled her from the chair. She didn't struggle or fight as he crushed his mouth to hers in a brutal kiss. He peeled the towel off her body, revealing her naked perfection.

He began trailing kisses along her jawline. Reaching her hands under his shirt, he pulled back to allow her to help him pull it over his head.

"My mate would never leave my side," she muttered as she trailed her fingernails down his chest, and lower. His abdomen muscles contracted at the feel of her touch.

"You would need a mate who is strong," he breathed. His hands gripped her breast as he tried to decide which one to taste first.

"He would need to accept me as a highborn because that's who I am." She gasped as he picked her up and tossed her onto the bed.

"He would have to respect you," Zeke murmured, unzipping his jeans. The heat in her eyes had his cock pushing painfully against his jeans.

He pushed his pants down, taking his boxer briefs with them. Crawling onto the bed, he got pleasure at seeing her immediately open her legs for him. He settled in-between her legs and instantly felt her heat on his belly. Their little game had him actually thinking that he could be the mate for her. Maybe it wouldn't be so bad. The sex between the two of them was off the charts, and from the little time that they had spent together, he could tell that they had much in common.

But there was one thing that he was forgetting.

This was destiny putting the two of them together. Destiny wouldn't put two people together without them being meant for each other. Destiny never made a mistake in deciding who should spend an eternity together. He thought of Ryan and Summer, Norrix and Emely, Remus and Ilena. They were all perfectly happy together, and none of them had been searching for a mate. Destiny brought them all together.

Small hands guided his face to hers. Her soft lips covered his and opened as his tongue pushed forth. Hers weren't shy at all and invited him in, deeper into her mouth. She tasted of sweet mint. His cock jumped, knowing that he was close to paradise. Placing her arms up over her head, he held them in place as he moved lower and began to feast on her breasts. He finally made up his mind.

The right one first.

The right one had a small mole right above her areola and it begged for him to kiss it first. He trailed his tongue around her mound before drawing it to her beaded nipple.

"Yes," she hissed, not fighting him. Her arms

remained up over her head as he bathed her plump mound with his tongue before moving over to the other one. "My mate will suck on my breasts to please me."

Her words caused him to lose all control. He sat up and pushed her legs open even wider, revealing her glistening pussy to him. He knew that she would be ready for him. Her pussy practically dripped as he lined the head of his cock up with her entrance.

"Say that you're mine," he demanded, slamming into her. His gums burned as his incisions burst through his gums. Nicia screamed as he stretched her. She was small and took all of him without complaint. Her walls contracted around him, causing him to grunt as he slid almost all the way out of her, leaving only the mushroom tip inside of her. "Say it."

She sat up on her elbows, her lust-filled eyes locked on his. He could see her incisors peeking from beneath her top lip. She reached up and pulled him on top of her, causing him to thrust inside of her again.

"I belong to you," she said, just as she pulled his head to the side, exposing his neck to her.

She sank her fangs directly into his vein. The feel of her feeding from him was unlike any other time a female vampire had drank from him before. A sharp bolt of lightening shot its way down his spine. He shouted as he began to thrust deep inside of her, his hips moving of their own accord. The feel of her lips was one of the most erotic feelings he had ever experienced.

"Fuck," he shouted, gripping the sheets tight as he thrust harder, trying to get even closer to her. "Nicia—"

It was like his hips were on autopilot. Every moan she let loose made him go faster. She wrapped her legs around his waist as he continued to pound his hard cock into her slippery channel. She pulled back from him, licking the wound closed with her tongue. Her head fell back, and he could see a slight tinge of blood on her lips.

"Claim me," she whispered. The look of pure pleasure on her face pulled him to her. There was no way that he would deny her. He knew that destiny did not make mistakes. Who was he to question what was written in the stars? He was a fool to think that he would never take a mate. Destiny had brought him the most perfect vampire.

"You're mine," he growled, pushing her face away from his to expose her neck. He had already drank from her once before and it hit him. It was because of the last time that they'd had sex, he'd created the bond between them when he couldn't avoid the temptation of tasting her sweet, thick blood. Destiny had revealed her as his mate from the moment they'd met.

Destiny sure was a sneaky bitch.

Zeke leaned in and dragged his tongue along her pounding artery. She smelled of fresh soap and woman—*his* woman. He sank his incisors deep into her neck, sealing them together for all eternity.

CHAPTER SIX

~ Zeke ~

Zeke would have to admit when he opened his eyes later that night, he didn't feel any different. It wasn't like something from the movies where he could notice a change. Music didn't play, birds didn't chirp in the background, and the world sure as hell didn't pause for him and Nicia. He felt like his same old self. Only this time, he was a mated vampire.

"There's something different about you," Remus noted, coming to lean against the car near Zeke.

"Fuck off," Zeke growled as Norrix joined them.

They were waiting for Nicia and her men to arrive. Tonight, they would hunt the last of the hunter's down and end this war. This time, Ryan didn't meet with the human officials and give them any information. According to Nicia's contact, there was a leak in the human government. They didn't know who, but someone was feeding the hunters information about the vampires.

"I see it too. If I didn't know any better, I would say it had something to do with the councilwoman," Norrix murmured. Zeke scowled at both of them. He knew it would come. They would both ride him hard for all the years he shunned mating.

"Something is wrong with your eyes." Zeke scowled, crossing his arms against his chest. He tried to ignore their snickers. He had broad shoulders and could easily handle their jokes.

"You know how he always said he would never mate?" Remus nudged Norrix.

"How could I forget?" Norrix snorted. "I think he rode you the hardest after you and Ilena mated."

"I did not." Zeke defended himself.

He was starting to rethink his friendship with the two. Mating with a female had made them both soft in the head. That had been his argument on why he would never mate. But with Nicia, it was different. He felt whole, and she didn't cause his brain to go to mush like the two vampires in front of him.

"You can stop denying it, Z," Remus stated, slapping Zeke on the shoulder. "There's nothing wrong with finding a mate."

"Okay, fine!" Zeke snapped, rolling his eyes.

"Yes, Nicia and I completed our mating bond."

He wouldn't be ashamed of his mate. She was a fierce vampire warrior. What man wouldn't be proud to know that his woman was strong and intelligent?

His words were met with silence as Norrix and Remus stared at him in disbelief.

"Wow," Norrix uttered as he stared at Zeke. "I never thought I would see the day."

The sound of crunching gravel alerted them that a vehicle was pulling into the driveway. Zeke pushed off the car as the vehicle came into view.

Nicia.

"She's just in time," Ryan announced as he came out of the front doors of the royal mansion. Zeke's eyes remained on the vehicle as it pulled up. It had been a few hours since he had last seen Nicia. He could still taste the sweetness of her on his tongue.

Ryan brushed past him and headed for the vehicle. Zeke did a double take at the king. He was dressed in an all leather outfit that covered his entire body. Only his head was free of the contraption.

"What the hell?" Zeke followed behind Ryan. He could feel Norrix and Remus stand behind him. The doors to the dark sedan opened and out stepped one of Nicia's guards who turned, went to the back passenger door and opened it. Nicia stepped from the car, dressed the same as Ryan.

"What are you wearing?" Norrix asked. Zeke's eyes took in Nicia dressed in the leather suit. Hers conformed to her body, displaying her perfect curves.

Her eyes met his and he could instantly feel a stirring beneath his belt, but he pushed those feelings to the side. They would have an eternity to explore each other and learn every facet of each other's bodies.

"This is a specialized treated vinyl and leather fabric to protect us from the sun," Nicia said, holding out her arms and turning in a slow circle.

"The sun?" Zeke glanced at the king before turning back to Nicia. What the hell was she talking about? They couldn't go into the sun. Vampires were allergic to the sun.

"Yes, the sun. We're going to attack the hunters when they least expect it," Nicia announced.

"In the morning." Ryan turned to them. Zeke could feel his eyebrows rise at the comment. Daylight? He couldn't even remember the last time he attempted to go out in daylight.

"Has this been tested?" Remus asked.

"Yes, it has." Nicia nodded her head. "We've used these a few times. You all asked how we have the hunters running from us? Well, here you go."

~ Nicia ~

Nicia could see the doubt in Zeke and the other's eyes. She glanced over at Stelios, Risto, and

Despina, and smirked. In the years that Ryan was gone, her and her team had made sure they used every resource that they had available to fight back. Her team of scientists had developed the suits to allow them to go out in the daytime.

With the addition of a facemask that covered their entire head, it allowed them to walk around on the brightest of days. That would be how they would defeat the hunters. They wouldn't expect vampires to attack during the day.

"It's a little snug," Remus said, stepping into the room, twisting around in a stretch.

They had provided each of the royal guards with a suit. If they were going to hunt the hunters, they would need to be ready, and fast. The sun would be rising soon.

"Give it time, it will stretch out," Risto said, walking over to the vampire and showing him how to fit the mask on.

Once the mask was on, no part of their skin would be visible for the sun's rays to burn. The eye covers provided protection from the UV rays. The suit itself would stretch and mold to the body of the person wearing it. Nicia never had any problems fighting in her suit.

Zeke stepped into the room with a scowl in place. Her breath caught in her throat at the sight of her mate in the form-fitting suit. Every vampire in the room was in top shape and the suits showed off their muscles, but Zeke took her breath away.

"How does it fit?" she asked as she stopped in

front of him. Her gums ached from her incisors wanting to descend. The thought of consuming his blood again came into her mind and she had to push it to the side.

Not now, she thought to herself.

They were about to embark on a battle to take out the rest of the hunters. Now was not the time to think of getting naked with her mate.

"Will I be able to fight in this?" he asked, stretching his arms high.

"The suit will learn your body. My scientists worked on these for years before getting it just right. Before the attacks, my father had been developing them. We were able to finish what he started," she said proudly. She wished her father were here to see his creation. Not only had he started this project, but many others as well. Her scientists were able to build on his legacy, and she was damn proud of him.

"Here, let me show you how to place the mask on properly," she offered, reaching for his.

She stepped closer to him and watched as his eyes darkened. She instantly knew that his thoughts were going down the same road as hers. He was too tall for her to reach up over his head, so he bent down a little, bringing his face closer to hers. Her core clenched as his eyes bored into hers, making her want to drag him into a nearby empty room and have her wicked way with him.

"Stop looking at me like that," she murmured.

"Look at you how?" he answered, his voice low.

She could feel eyes on her back and knew that everyone in the room was watching them. She knew that Despina was curious of Zeke. She had told her friend that she and Zeke had officially mated. Her longtime friend's mouth had just about hit the floor when she broke the news to her.

She ignored his question as she stretched the headpiece out and proceeded to pull it down over his head. It snapped in place with little snaps that were placed around the base of the neck. She stepped back and nodded.

"Move around and let the material get to know you," she instructed to Zeke and the other guards.

"Nicia, these are perfect," Ryan said as he walked around the room, assessing his men. She had given him his suit earlier before she'd left. "Your father would be proud of you."

"I know, and thank you." Her father would have loved to see his suits being used for the good of vampires. She walked around with Ryan, ensuring that all the vampires were comfortable. A few of them practiced fighting moves, allowing the material to conform to them.

Pleased with what she saw, she turned to Ryan with a devilish smile spreading across her face. "Let's go end this war."

CHAPTER SEVEN

~ Nicia ~

The sun would be rising soon, and the vampires were making their way to the hunters' headquarters. The hunters were hidden deep in a rural area. From Nicia's experience with them, attacking them during the day would take them by surprise. This was not the first time that Nicia and her warriors had attacked humans during the day. Their suits would perform perfectly.

The humans would be no match for the vampires in full hand-to-hand combat. That's why they had to develop their special weapons over time to try to get the upper hand over vampires. But no longer would they be the top of the food chain. Vampires would rise again, and with Nicia and Ryan siding together, it was guaranteed that this would be the outcome.

Nicia had been keeping a tab on the hunters and their activities. Even though she was pissed at Ryan for his reappearance, she almost stepped in when they had kidnapped his mate, Summer. She had yet to meet Summer, and from what Nicia had heard, it was Summer who convinced Ryan to come forward and reveal himself. Nicia couldn't wait to meet the queen and thank her for having him come home. With the king's return, it created a fire in the vampires. It gave them hope, and for that, Nicia was grateful to her.

They quickly made it through the woods and stood on the edge of the hunter's compound. A few buildings had been erected to act as their headquarters. The humans had completely kept themselves off the grid, and that was why even their own government didn't know where they were. Nicia's eyes assessed the grounds in the early morning light.

She always got a rush at being out in the daytime. On dreary days and no sun, vampires could be out during the daylight without fear of their skin burning. On bright and sunny days, vampires would not risk venturing out into the sun. Third degree burns were quite painful.

"I don't see anyone," Ryan said, coming to stand beside her. The air was quiet, but Nicia knew that the humans would just be stirring.

"They're here," she murmured as her eyes caught movement on the other side of the property.

"There's nothing special about these buildings. Risto was able to research them. No basements.

"No surprises." Ryan nodded in understanding.

The vampires had spread out around the property. The humans who had attacked Ryan and his vampires were getting cocky. They would not expect the vampires to be here in the day. The hunters in her area had long ago pulled out, seeing that Nicia and her vampires were too strong and fought back. She'd had the hunters running. She refused to lay down and be exterminated like roaches.

Zeke came to stand on her other side, and it took everything she had not to look his way. Outfitted with weapons made him one dangerous vampire, and her body had certainly taken notice.

"None of them are to live," he growled. Her pussy literally contracted at his words. She knew her mate was a fierce warrior, and his fierce nature just did it for her.

"The human government has given us free reign to do what we want," Ryan said. Her head snapped toward him at his words. That was unlike the human officials. "They don't support any of the works of the hunters anymore. This was the agreement in trying to restore the relations between humans and vampires. We can bring them in dead or alive."

"So, what are we, their bounty hunters?" Nicia snapped. She'd be damned if she worked for the humans. Let them do their own damn work.

"This is part of the treaty. No humans are to hunt down any vampires. Killing an innocent vampire will be cause for punishment by the vampire king, is how it is worded."

"Death it is, My King," she breathed around her fangs as she turned her eyes back to the compound.

Yes, it was time for the hunted to hunt the hunter.

~ Zeke ~

Zeke had to make himself stay focused. Nicia in all of her weapons and leather body suit was enough to make him come in his own suit. The sword strapped to her back was a sign that she was not a vampire to mess with. The three of them approached the main house. Each vampire group would converge on a different building. Nicia knew that the two-story home would hold the leader of the hunters.

He was still amazed that they were able to walk outside in the sun with the suits on and nothing happened. His skin didn't even tingle. The suits were really doing their job. Nicia had been right. The material molded to his body perfectly. He almost couldn't tell it was on him. The leather was supple and soft, and created a protective layer for them. The mask would be a thing to get used to wearing, but it would be worth it if it meant bringing an end to the hunters.

Zeke's fangs pushed through his gums. Just the thought of taking out the lowlife humans had him in a rage. His people had suffered at the hands of the hunters for too long. With the new treaty, and taking out the leader of the hunters, it would send the rest of the hunters running. Not having the government support was a low blow too. Before, these humans were allowed to kill a vampire with no repercussions.

Nicia quickly picked the lock and let them in the house. They silently made their way into the building. Nicia held her handgun in her hand, pointing it ahead as she led them into the building. He would have preferred to be in front, but she threw daggers at him from her eyes when he tried to move in front of her.

The need to protect her burned in his chest.

The house was quiet at a tomb. Nicia motioned that she would go upstairs, and for them to check out the rest of the house.

He shook his head. Not happening. He was going with her. Ryan motioned for Zeke to go with her and he would check out the first floor. He tightened his grip on his weapon as he followed her up the stairs. They took their time, trying to ensure that their footsteps remained silent.

At the top was a hallway with a few doors that were closed. Zeke narrowed his eyes.

Something was off.

Shouldn't the humans be awake by now? The

sun was up. He didn't like the feeling that was in the pit of his stomach. He pushed in front of her, not caring that she would be pissed. She kept silent, but he could feel the heat of her gaze on his back.

He stepped to the first door and slowly opened it. It was a bedroom, with a twin bed in the corner. The room was untouched. Zeke slowly crept in with his gun trained on the closed door that was across from the bed that he assumed was the closet. He quickly ripped the door open and it was empty as well.

He turned and walked out the door to find that Nicia had just checked the room across the hall. She shook her head as she came to the doorway.

Two more rooms.

Warning sirens wailed in the back of his mind. Something was not right, but they had to find Stanley Kohl. They could not leave without him dying.

Nicia moved to the next door. He looked over her shoulder and saw that it was an empty bathroom. No hidden surprises. He moved past her and placed his hand on the knob and turned. He slowly pushed the door open with his gun raised.

He sucked in his breath as a force slammed into his chest, tossing him to the floor.

CHAPTER EIGHT

~ Nicia ~

Nicia cursed as she rushed to Zeke's fallen body. The sight of him being thrown back against the wall left her heart in her throat. The front of his suit was smoking where the bullet entered his chest. The faint blue light radiating from his chest caught her eyes.

Solaris.

Anger mounted at the sight. The hunters shouldn't have these deadly bullets anymore. Zeke's head rolled to the side as she snatched the head mask from him, revealing his closed eyes.

She reached up to feel for a pulse, but the sound of a rifle cocking behind her caused her hand to pause. She crumpled the mask in her hand as she slowly turned.

Stanley Kohl stood inside the bedroom with a modified shotgun aimed at her. She snatched her mask from her face and brandished her fangs.

The human would die.

A growl escaped her chest as she stood from her spot.

"Now you stay right there, vampire," Stanley warned, his rifle following her as she stood to her full height.

Footsteps stomped up the stairs and she threw her hand up to warn Ryan. She didn't take her eyes off the human.

"Or what?" she bit out around her fangs. She dropped the masks from her hands and flexed her fingers, trying to think of which weapon she would use to kill the hunter.

"You're going to get pumped full of this Solaris. You think they took it all from us? Who do you think came up with the idea?" he bragged.

"You may shoot and kill me with those bullets, but I hope you have enough to take out a vampire army," she hissed, taking a step toward him.

He had shot her mate with the deadly bullets, and for this, he would pay. She needed her men to get up here to save Zeke, but there was no way for her to alert them.

She could feel Ryan creep toward her, but she would be damned if she'd let him get shot and killed. He was needed for their people. She may have been pissed at him for his disappearing act, but truth was, he was the king, and he would lead their people.

"Stop!" Stanley shouted, waving the rifle in his hand frantically. "How the hell are you walking around in the daytime without burning?"

Her eyes narrowed on the human. Vampires were much faster than them, so even if he got a shot off, there was no way he would make it out of the house alive.

"Don't come any closer!" he screamed, backing up further into the room. He was trapped and he knew it. His eyes grew frantic as she took another step. "I have the shades opened!" he threatened, but it was no use. The only thing that would be exposed to the rays of the sun was her head, and right now, that was the least of her worries. She would heal.

"Your men are probably already dead," she stated, taking another step into the room. She'd be willing to die for her people. She just needed to get far enough into the room to shut the door. Once the door was shut, she hoped that Ryan would be able to drag Zeke out of the house. If her men could get to him in time, they would be able to save him.

Sacrificing herself for him would be worth it.

She loved him.

She balked at the idea, but knew that it was true.

"I said stop fucking walking!" he hollered. This time, he aimed the rifle at her chest.

She used her vampire speed to slam the door shut. Time seemed to stand still as she quickly advanced on the human. The sound of the rifle going off filled the air. She dodged the bullet and advanced. Her hand reached for her sword strapped to her back and she swung it toward Stanley, hitting the rifle and slicing it in half. She whipped around and thrust the sword behind her, hitting her target.

She turned to find the stunned human with her sword embedded in his abdomen. The handle of the broken rifle fell to the floor as his knees gave out. She smirked as she stood before the human. His eyes were glassed over as they stared up at her. A trail of blood escaped from his mouth as he tried to form words, but failed.

What better way to send this human to hell than for him to be ended by the thing he hated most? She snatched his head to the side, baring his neck. She would gladly bleed this fucker dry for all the decimation he had caused her people.

"There will be someone else after me," he gasped.

"Then we'll just have to kill them too," she snapped, sinking her fangs into his throat.

Nicia ran down the stairs, following the sounds of shouting. Her body hummed with the new energy from the human's blood. She'd bled him dry, and he would never cause another vampire trouble again. She knew that Stelios would be able to help Zeke. She prayed they weren't too late.

She rushed into the living room and found Zeke on the floor, surrounded by others. She brushed past the men and knelt beside her mate's still body. They had ripped the suit from his chest in order to get to the bullet's entry site. His chest held a single bullet hole that singed the skin. The skin surrounding the hole was burned. The chemical in the bullets were made from a substance that mimicked the sun's rays and burned vampires from the inside out once the solution entered the bloodstream of a vampire.

"How is he?" she asked Stelios as he withdrew a syringe from Zeke's chest.

Once the hunters began using Solaris, her scientists had obtained a few of the bullets and were able to create an agent that could block the chemical. The only caveat was that they had to introduce it to the vampire's bloodstream immediately in order for it to work.

"We'll know shortly," he murmured, concentrating on his patient.

She bit her lip as she waited for her guard to work on her mate. She wished she could go back upstairs and draw out the death of the human and torture him like he should have been for what he had done to vampires.

"What did you just give him?" Ryan demanded, standing over them with his face full of concern.

"It's an agent that should block the Solaris," Stelios announced to the room.

Gasps filled the room as Ryan and his vampires

paused their chatter and looked at them.

"How long have you had this?" Norrix's voice appeared behind her.

"A few months," Nicia said, her eyes not leaving Zeke's still face. She sent up a prayer to every deity that she could think of to save her mate. "Zeke, can you hear me?" she whispered, moving closer to run her fingers through his hair.

The agent had to work. Panic filled her chest with the thought that she would lose him after just finding him. Destiny wouldn't be that cruel...would she?

"Now we wait." Stelios sat back from Zeke's body.

"How will we know if it works?" Remus asked.

"If he doesn't die," Risto murmured as he moved to stand behind Stelios.

The room fell quiet as they all waited to see what Zeke would do—take his last breath, or open his eyes.

"Don't you die on me, Zeke," she demanded as her eyes filled with tears. She grabbed his hand in hers and squeezed. She needed to let him feel that she was near and fighting for him. Their mating bond had to mean something to destiny. "You big, stubborn vampire. I need you," she whispered, her voice ending on a squeak.

She jumped back as Zeke took a sharp intake of breath. Her heart slammed against her chest as she waited. The room drew quiet as everyone waited to see if the medication would work. His chest slowly fell and she leaned forward, frantic. This couldn't be it. He couldn't be taking his last breath. This wasn't to be their future. She refused to believe it.

A single tear fell from her face as she leaned over him. His eyes slowly fluttered. She held her breath as he opened his hazel eyes. His hand squeezed hers as he stared into her eyes.

"I need you too."

EPILOGUE

~ Nicia ~

"The war is over," Ryan said from his chair into the camera. The room was filled with people in charge of making sure this broadcast was viewed all over the world. "Vampires will no longer run from the hunters. We will rebuild. We will exist alongside humans in harmony and peace as we once did in the days of my father."

Nicia stood off to the side of the office near the door as she watched her longtime friend and his mate address the vampire nation, and humans, on television in front of the massive fireplace in his office. She had finally got to meet Summer, and loved the vampire queen. She was perfect for Ryan. Nicia and Summer immediately hit it off and were becoming fast friends.

Her chest filled with pride that they were finally at a place where they could live in peace and start thinking of the future without the thought of war.

That fateful day where she thought she had lost her mate, they had succeeded in bringing an end to the hunters. Not only did they kill the last remaining members, but they destroyed everything in the compound that could be used against vampires. The hunters would hunt no more.

A warm body pressed up against her from behind, causing her breath to catch in her throat.

Zeke.

Her heart rate sped up with the sheer presence of her mate being near. Ever since he woke up, they had been unable to keep their hands off each other. The last week, they had come to the realization that the universe was much bigger than them.

She glanced back up at him and smiled, gripping his larger hand in hers. This stubborn vampire was hers for all eternity.

"Any council members or heirs to the council who are out there, I urge you to come forward. If we, as a vampire nation, are to make any strides into the future to rebuild our great nation, we will need you."

That was their cue to come forward. Together, they would show unity between the royal family and council. Together, Ryan and Nicia would work to build their people up again. The future looked promising.

Zeke and Nicia moved to stand behind the royal

couple so that they would be in the shot. She rested her hand on Ryan's shoulder as she peered into the camera. Vampires everywhere would be watching them.

"Join us," she said with a warm smile on her face.

~ The End ~

ABOUT THE AUTHOR

Ariel Marie is an author who loves the paranormal, action and hot steamy romance. She combines all three in each and every one of her stories. For as long as she can remember, she has loved vampires, shifters and every creature you can think of. This even rolls over into her favorite movies! She loves a good action packed thriller! Throw a touch of the supernatural world in it and she's hooked!

She grew up in Cleveland, Ohio where she currently resides with her husband and three beautiful children.

Connect with Ariel Marie online!

www.facebook.com/authorarielmarie
www.twitter.com/the_ArielMarie
www.thearielmarie.com

ACKNOWLEDGMENTS

I would like to take the time to say thank you to everyone who has purchased a book from me. It still amazes me that someone wants to read my books!

To my editor, beta team, street team and advanced reader team, thank you! I couldn't do what I do without you.

To my family—I love you! Being able to following a dream in life with you all right there by my side, makes me feel all warm and fuzzy on the inside.

I hope everyone has enjoyed the Vampire Destiny box set. I had so much fun putting it together. Don't be shy; let me know if you liked this series!

Until next time,

Ariel Marie

ALSO BY
ARIEL MARIE

The Dark Shadows Series
Princess
Toma
Phaelyn
Teague
Adrian
Nicu

The Mirrored Prophecy Series
Power of the Fae
Fight for the Fae
Future of the Fae (TBD)

Stand Alone Books
Dani's Return
A Faery's Kiss

Anthologies
Fourteen Shades of F*cked Up: An Anthology
Claiming My Valentine: An Anthology

When Clubs Collide: An MC Anthology

Made in the USA
Columbia, SC
04 September 2018